# A Death in the Family

by

Geoff Collins

This book is a work of fiction. Names, characters, places and incidents are either the product of the author's imagination or are used fictitiously. Any resemblance to actual persons, living or dead, or to actual events or locales is entirely coincidental.

**A DEATH IN THE FAMILY**
**Copyright © 2019 Geoff Collins** All rights reserved, including the right to reproduce this book, or portions thereof, in any form. No part of this text may be reproduced, transmitted, downloaded, decompiled, reverse engineered, or stored in or introduced into any information storage and retrieval system, in any form or by any means, whether electronic or mechanical without the express written permission of the author. The scanning, uploading, and distribution of this book via the Internet or via any other means without the permission of the author and publisher is illegal and punishable by law. Please purchase only authorized electronic editions and do not participate in or encourage electronic piracy of copyrighted materials.

The publisher does not have any control over and does not assume any responsibility for author or third-party websites or their content.

Front cover designed by Geoff Collins

Front cover art: © Mangojuicy | Dreamstime.com File ID: 13334285
Back cover art: © Mangojuicy | Dreamstime.com File ID: 13334285
Interior art—coffin illustration Pixabay License Free for commercial use
Interior art—dog illustration Pixabay CC0 Creative Commons Free for commercial use

Interior art—Prime Suspects illustration Shutterstock.com **File ID**: 58681264

Edited by Joe Gartrell and Ben Gibson of Word Mule. www.wordmule.com

Published by A & J Publishing, LLC
3266 Hartwell Street
Johns Island, SC 29455

Visit the author website: www.booksbycollins.com

Categories: FICTION / Thrillers / Crime

ISBN: 978-1-948046-90-9 (eBook)
ISBN: 978-1-948046-91-6 (Paperback)

Version: 2019.10.29

*To my friends at Project Paw Alive and the many other police and military K-9 organizations and support groups.*

*A special thanks to Joe Gartrell and Ben Gibson of Word Mule.*
www.wordmule.com

*This book is dedicated to ...*

# Art Collins

## *Nick Giordano Novels*

**"A Holy City Mystery Artfully Spun"**

*Geoff Collins is a wonderfully versatile writer (check out his bibliography), and here, he weaves a delightful mystery set in the Holy City. Hop along and crack this case with Giordano—you won't regret, and it will get you primed for the other books coming along in the series.*

**"Well Written ... Interesting Characters and Plenty of Suspense"**

*Good mystery with interesting characters and plenty of suspense. A cybersecurity expert is hired to determine if narcotics theft is taking place at Charleston SC hospital and who is behind it. Well written with lots of fascinating details.*

**"Wonderfully Crafted Story Set in Charleston"**

*Wonderfully crafted story set in Charleston, SC—great story line and vivid imagery. Collins follows Giordano with insight and honesty. Can't wait for Nick's next adventure.*

## "A Fast and Exciting Read"

*The books are a fast read. Exciting and held my interest throughout. Hope to see more from this author.*

## "Another Wild Ride"

*Tools of the Trade takes us on another wild ride with Nick Giordano and his crew. Collins, as he did with his previous book in this three-part series, deftly weaves on intricate story line that builds to a satisfying, thrilling end. Highly recommend Collins, a writer who deserves a vast readership.*

## "Excitement and Suspense"

*Excitement and suspense as mafia and white supremacists fight over the drug market in Charleston SC. Characters well-developed and interesting story line.*

## "A Lowcountry Mystery"

*In this series, which sadly wraps here with Book Three, Collins found a higher gear with each, serving up a fresh batch of nasty folks for the series' core characters to root out and take down. That the books were set in Charleston only added to their delight. The only rotten aspect here is that this is the last we'll see of Nick Giordano and his pals—that is, unless, this crew comes around for cameos in one of Collins' future works. Hats off!*

*"If you're going to do something, do it well,
and leave something witchy."*
**–Charles Manson**


*"I'm the most cold-hearted son-of-a-bitch you'll ever meet."*
**–Ted Bundy**


*"Even psychopaths have emotions; then again, maybe not."*
**–Richard Ramirez**

# A DEATH IN THE FAMILY

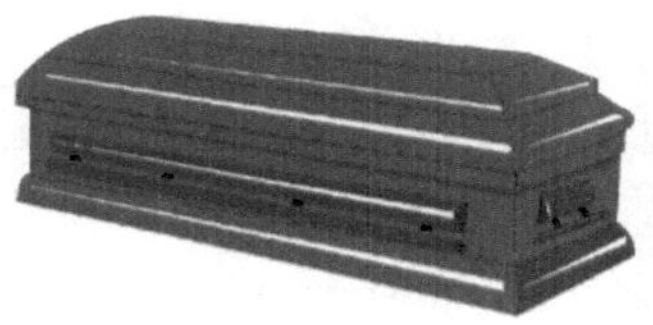

# CHAPTER ONE

Thursday, March 1

HARSH WHITE LIGHT bathed the cramped interview room, about the size of a guestroom closet in an oceanfront house on Isle of Palms. Adam Stone leaned against the slate-gray wall next to the two-way mirror watching his partner Marcus Williams interrogate Devon Jackson.

"Hey, Devon, I've been wondering. Is your old lady still hookin'?"

A hint of a smile crossed Devon's face, but he said nothing. It wasn't the first time he'd played the game.

A member of the Bloods, Jackson ran the gang's drug business in the Ashford area of North Charleston. He'd been recruited into the gang at the tender age of eleven—but there was nothing tender about him. His story was all too common; dropped out of school, single mom working two jobs, father long gone. He had nothing close to a normal childhood. The street robbed him of that. He was pushing dime bags at thirteen, carrying heat at fourteen, running his own crew at sixteen. At seventeen, he'd already been in and out of the system numerous times. Detective Stone knew Devon would have no qualms about putting a bullet right between his eyes.

Jackson had been picked up a few days earlier on possession with intent to sell. Charleston's heroin and fentanyl activity had increased over the last year, resulting in a string of major crackdowns. Stone headed up the task force that had just raided one of the larger distribution houses in North Charleston. The raid resulted in the death of Cedric Salazar, the head of the Bloods' drug distribution network in the Charleston area.

Stone and Williams had both spent almost twenty years on the force, the last five as partners. They were members of the elite Organized Crime Unit (OCU) of Captain Ed Merchant's Special Operations Division. From the beginning of their partnership, they consistently topped the department's "kill" chart, which tracked the successful completion of investigations.

The two could not have looked more different or come from more divergent backgrounds. Stone was white, 5' 11" and 185. Williams was black, 6' 4", topping the scales at 250. Williams' face was all hard edges—like it was whittled from a block of mahogany. Stone's longish light blond hair was in stark contrast to his partner's shaved charcoal-black head.

Williams dressed in dark blue suits, his tie always knotted, his gold detective badge clipped to his leather belt. Stone preferred jeans and a sport coat, and Williams was always on him about it.

"Christ, Adam, you look like a 90s stand-up comic. If you're going to wear tennis shoes, at least get a pair that aren't rotting off your feet."

Stone would glance down at his scuffed Adidas and think about making a trip to the mall where some twelve-year-old-looking kid would try to sell him a pair of $300 Air Jordan Retros. *The Adidas were probably good for a few more months—at least.*

Raised in Charleston's predominantly white, affluent suburb of Mt. Pleasant, Adam enjoyed the fruits of the upper-middle class. Marcus—not so much. He grew up in North Charleston's tough Union Heights neighborhood. His mom, a single parent, worked two jobs to put food on the table and cover rent for their small two-bedroom apartment.

They did, however, share something in common—sports. Marcus excelled on the football field, while Adam nailed three-pointers on the basketball court. A full ride to Clemson University was Marcus' ticket out of the ghetto, probably the only thing that saved him from going the Devon Jackson route.

Adam's roundball prowess wasn't enough to land him a spot on a major college team, but he did enjoy four years of moderate success as a shooting guard at Francis Marion University. He continued to play ball in a highly competitive downtown Charleston league, and he hit the court every Saturday morning at the gym. After over twenty years on the court, the guys he played against seemed to be getting bigger, faster, and younger—as his aches mounted and speed dwindled. But at forty-one, Adam Stone could still hold his own against the young bucks. Marcus would sometimes join Adam on the court, but it was clear he preferred tackling over guarding his opponents.

Stone slowly eased himself off the wall and said, "Devon, you want something to drink?"

"Coke," responded Jackson without looking up.

"Damn," Stone drawled with exaggerated regret, "I just remembered the machine's broke."

No reaction.

They'd been grilling Jackson for almost two hours straight trying to find out who was supplying the Bloods with the fentanyl-laced heroin. He barely spoke—consistently answering the detectives' questions with a simple "no," "yeah," or "don't know." Until, finally, he divulged a little extra: "I gotta take a piss."

Stone turned to his partner. "Hey Marcus, did they fix that toilet yet?"

"Nope. Still busted."

Jackson mumbled, "Fuck you, Stone, guess I'll just piss on the fucking floor then. Smells like someone already did."

Stone leaned forward. "That's disrespectful, Devon. If I were you, I'd watch your fucking language."

Jackson slowly lifted his head and stared at Stone—his eyes dark with menace. "If I were you, detective, I'd watch your fucking back. We know you triggered Cedric."

He was right. In the melee of the North Charleston raid, Stone had, in fact, shot and killed Cedric Salazar. Salazar was the Blood's boss or shot caller. Revenge ran deep in the Bloods' DNA—Stone knew the threat was real.

Marcus was visually irritated. He leaned back and warned Jackson, "You better watch your ass and don't threaten …"

But before he could finish, there was a knock on the door, and an officer stuck his head in the room. "Detective Stone, you've got a phone call."

Adam was perturbed. "Take a message."

"Sorry, sir, but you probably need to take this one."

Stone glanced at his watch and saw that it was almost 6:00. "All right let's take a break. Marcus, let Devon take a piss and get him something to drink."

As soon as he got to the bullpen, he saw another detective holding the phone for him and took it. "Detective Stone."

"Mr. Stone, this is Jenny Black at Charleston Collegiate. I've got your daughter here in my office. We'll be closing up here pretty soon, and Mrs. Stone hasn't been by yet to pick her up." The school had an after-school program that Stone's twelve-year-old daughter, Piper, attended Monday through Friday.

"Did you call my wife?"

"Yes, sir. We called her office and cell. She didn't answer either."

"Huh, sorry about that. She probably got tied up with one of her patients. She turns her phone off when she's in session.

I'll give her mother, Mrs. Kendell, a call. She's on your list to get Piper. Either way, one of us will be by shortly."

Adam's wife, Ann, was a psychologist with a small practice on Savannah Highway and normally picked up Piper around 5:30. Even though she sometimes had to deal with patient emergencies, it was extremely unusual for her to be late, especially without giving notice. Adam's hours were unpredictable—often requiring him to work late into the night. Because of that, Ann had limited her practice to only four days a week so she could be there for their daughter.

Concern registered on Adam's radar when he called Ann's mom.

Tracy Kendell answered the phone and Adam said, "Hi, Tracy. I need a favor. Ann must have got tied up with one of her patients and lost track of time. She hasn't been by to pick up Piper yet. She's still at school. Can you get her? I'll swing by after work and pick her up."

"Sure, dear, I'm on my way now." It wasn't the first time Tracy picked up Piper when Ann was running late.

Adam thanked her before he dove back into the interrogation dance he'd been through with Marcus hundreds of times before. Devon remained stoic and unresponsive, occasionally defiant. The routine played out in predictable fashion for another hour before Adam took a call from Tracy. "Adam, I'm worried. I've been trying Ann every fifteen minutes or so, and she's still not answering."

Stone had been focused on the interrogation, but now his concern shifted. "All right. I'm leaving the station now. I'll be there in about half an hour." He hung up and pulled Marcus out of the interrogation room. "Listen, I need to take off. Ann's MIA. Probably just busy at work but do me a favor. Just to be on the safe side, check if there's been any traffic accidents around James Island. Also, call the hospitals. Give me a buzz and let me know what you find out."

"You got it," Marcus said. "And I'll send Devon back to the detention center. We'll deal with his ass tomorrow."

~~~~

Ann's office was in an old house on Savannah Highway that had been converted into office space. Dr. Kate Shaw, a clinical psychiatrist and friend of Ann's, had her practice on the ground floor of the same converted house. They each had private entrances—Ann's in the rear of the building that led up to her second-floor office.

Pulling into the small parking lot behind the house, Adam noticed Ann's Fiat was gone. He had an office key and let himself in. A few lights were on, but outside of that—things seemed normal—bland and beige and soothing. Even the seascapes hanging on the walls seemed selectively non-threatening—no stormy skies or turbulent seas. The office had a small carpeted waiting room consisting of three dark leather chairs and a few glass tables on which the usual array of generic waiting room magazines were neatly arranged. The whole area felt designed not to trigger those on the brink.
~~~~

There was a small restroom off the hallway leading to a larger room that Ann used to meet with her patients. Her calendar was open on her desk, and the only thing she had scheduled that day was a three o'clock appointment with their tax accountant, Bill Bennett. Bennett handled Ann's business tax filings as well as their personal returns.

The days of therapists taking hand-written session notes were long past. Most used an iPad to record their observations. It was not unusual for Ann to clear a day in order to consolidate her session notes and transfer them to the individual patient folders on her office's main computer. Finding nothing out of the ordinary, Adam left her office, locking the door behind him.

Ten minutes later, he pulled into Tracy's driveway and was about to get out when Marcus called. You could hear the apprehension in his voice when Adam asked, "What did you find out?"

"Nothing really. She hasn't been involved in any accidents as far as I can tell. I contacted Roper, MUSC, Mercy, and all the emergency clinics. No record of Ann being admitted. What do you want me to do?"

Adam thought for a moment. "Let Chief Taylor know what's up. I know it's only been a few hours, but this isn't like Ann. I've called her cell several times, and it keeps going to message. Ask the chief if he could put out an APB on her car. It's a lime green 2015 Fiat 500. I don't remember the plate number, but you can look it up."

"You got it, brother. I'm sure there's some simple explanation. Cell battery probably just ran out or something. Let me know if I can do anything else to help."

"Thanks, Marcus. You're probably right." Despite his casual response, some frightening thoughts began to materialize. *Where the hell could she be? If she'd gotten in a car accident, it would have been reported. She had been a little distant lately, and that was probably his fault. Too many missed dinners and late nights at the station. They both had busy lives. After fourteen years of marriage, he'd seen a few of their friends split up. Could Ann be seeing someone else? Not a chance. But where was she?*

Adam rapped on Tracy's door three times before letting himself in. Piper was on the living room floor in front of the television—an untouched sandwich and glass of milk on the coffee table next to her. "Dad, Granny said Mom's working late. When's she coming home?"

"I don't know, sweetheart. Let's head on home. Maybe she's there already."

"Can I watch the end of my show? Please. It's only ten more minutes."

That was fine with Adam. It would give him a few moments to talk to Tracy in private. "Sure. I'll be with Granny in the kitchen."

Tracy was staring out the window over the sink, her hands clutching the counter—her unease and concern clear. "Any news?"

"Not yet. Maybe she had car problems, and her cell battery died. You know she always forgets to charge that thing. Even so, I let the chief know. He's having someone look into it."

"I don't know what to do, Adam. Ann always calls me if she's going to be late getting Piper."

Her head shook. He could only imagine what was going through it. Probably some of the same worst-case scenarios running through his own mind, thoughts that were becoming increasingly hard to suppress as the anxious minutes ticked by.

"It's okay, Tracy."

She peeled her hands from the counter and turned to give him a hug.

"Ann's fine," he said, "I promise. When we hear her explanation, we'll all probably have a good laugh."

~~~~

The Stones lived in James Island's Seaside Plantation, only five minutes from Tracy's. As soon as they were back at their house, Adam stepped onto the back patio to call two of Ann's closest friends. His heart sank when he learned neither had heard from her. He then dialed Bill Bennett, who sounded a bit perturbed when he picked up and said Ann wasn't there when he got to her office for their three o'clock. He'd tried calling her and waited around for about a half hour before he gave up and left.

It was almost 8:30 and still no word from Ann.

"Dad, when's Mom getting home?"
~~~~

"I don't know, sweetheart. Hopefully, she'll be home soon. You know sometimes she has to see her patients at the hospital. Go ahead and get ready for bed. You can read for a half hour, but then it's lights out."

An hour later, Adam had Piper in bed and settled down. Like most nights, Max, their black lab mix, was curled up with her.

Still no word on Ann. He called the station. Chief Taylor was gone for the day, and he spoke to the desk sergeant. "Nothing yet, detective. Chief had me send a shout-out to all the patrols before he left. I'll call if I hear anything."

Adam's anxiety was growing, but there wasn't much he could do but wait and hope. The hours dragged on. No word. Tracy phoned several times, and each time he told her the same—no news. The silence was an incubator for the worst kinds of dread. It was after midnight when Marcus called to tell Adam he'd again checked all the hospitals in Charleston. No luck.

~~~~

*Her eyes fluttered. A wave of nausea washed over her as the effects of the drug began to subside. She shivered. Cold, so cold. She felt something touch her face, and her head was gently pulled back.*

*And then a voice—hollow like it was coming from deep within a tunnel. "Time to go to heaven."*

*The knife slid across her throat, and then came the darkness.*
~~~~

# CHAPTER TWO
### Friday, March 2

ADAM'S EYES WERE fixed on his iPhone clock—2:00 a.m., 3:00 a.m., 4:00 a.m.—nothing. Why wasn't she answering her phone? Her car was gone. She must have driven somewhere. But where? Or did she ever even make it to her office? He felt helpless, and Devon Jackson's words kept coming back to him: *If I were you, detective, I'd watch your fucking back. We know you triggered Cedric.* Could the Bloods have taken Ann?

He tried to mask that dark thought with memories of their first date and the life they'd shared together. The memories came and went like a kaleidoscope. He had to smile when he remembered when a friend at the department tried to convince him to go on a blind date with this "nice girl" he knew. As far as Adam was concerned, the phrase, "nice girl" didn't sound too promising. But after several "thanks, but no thanks" declarations, he finally agreed.

He'd never forget the first time he laid eyes on that "nice girl." And it wasn't just the fact that she was drop dead gorgeous. There was something more—the warmth of her smile, the electricity of her touch. And then there were her eyes—clear and bright with a certain undefinable sparkle. They were alluring and sensual, mischievous, too. It had been more than fifteen years since he'd first looked into those eyes. Age had started painting its fine lines, and the crow's feet were beginning to show. But their glow remained, as did the promise of more tomorrows.

Eventually, the gray light of dawn began to seep through the living room window, and the dark images returned.

~~~~

"Piper, up and at 'em. It's 6:30 already. Get dressed, and I'll get you some breakfast."

Piper rolled over in bed. "Is Mom home?"

"Not yet, sweetheart. Hurry up now."

Thirty minutes later, Adam had Piper dressed, fed, and at the bus stop. "Have a good day, dear. I gotta get to work."

"Love you, Dad."

"Love you more."
~~~~

Adam started back to the house when Piper called out to him, "Dad, did something happen to Mom?"

"I don't know, sweetheart. I'll bet she had an emergency with one of her patients. Remember, that happened before, and she had to stay at the hospital all night with them. Don't worry, I'm sure she's fine. I'll let you know as soon as she comes home."

As the bus drove away, Adam could see her face through the rear window. It was clear Piper knew something was wrong.

Forty minutes later, Adam was seated in Chief Dan Taylor's office. Captain Ed Merchant was also there. "Adam, you look like hell," Merchant said.

"I feel like hell, Ed. Didn't sleep. I know it's been less than a day, but something's happened to Ann. Hell, she never came home last night."

"When's the last time you saw her?" Taylor asked.

"Yesterday morning. Around 7:30. She left for her office about the same time I did."

"Did you talk to her at all yesterday?"

"No, not after she left for work. She usually picks up our daughter after school but never made it there yesterday. I stopped by her office on the way to get my daughter. I found her calendar, and the only thing she had scheduled was a meeting with the guy that does her taxes. She clears her schedule every week or two to catch up with paperwork. I called the tax guy last night, and he said when he got to her office at three, she wasn't there."

Chief Taylor thought for a moment. "Adam, you know I gotta ask. Have you two been okay?"

"We're fine. No problems."

"Any arguments lately?" Taylor asked.

"Nothing really. Hell, Dan, we've been married fourteen years. We've had our ups and downs—but honestly, everything's solid between us. Listen, something happened to her yesterday. I feel it."

"How's she been lately? Has she been acting different? How about work? She's got a pretty stressful job. Has she ever spent the night at someone else's house? Has she ever done that?"

"No, Chief, none of that. She always lets me know if something's really bothering her."

Taylor picked up his phone and punched in a few numbers. "Mary, are Claire and Matt in? Good. Tell them I want to see them. Yes, now." He hung up. "All right, Adam, I'm giving this to Detectives Charles and Manson." Claire Charles and Matt Manson had been partnered together for the last few years. As you can imagine, it didn't take long before everyone began referring to the duo as simply "Charles Manson."

"Thanks, Chief. I appreciate it."

"One more thing," Taylor said. "They'll be working this— not you. You'll obviously be giving them information on Ann. If they need you to do something, then do it. But stay out of their way. Do we understand each other?"

"Chief, it's my wife we're talking about."

"Yes, and that's why. You've been doing this long enough to know how it works. They're going to have to treat you as a suspect until they can clear you. I know you had nothing to do with Ann's disappearance, but we need to do this by the book. I also know that's asking a lot, but that's the way it's got to be. Again, do we understand each other?"

Adam paused and took a deep breath. "Yes, sir," he said, knowing there was no way he was staying on the sideline with Ann out there somewhere.

There was a knock, and Detectives Charles and Manson entered. Both nodded to Adam.

"Sit down," Taylor said. "We have a situation."

Adam and Charles Manson met in one of the small conference rooms. Claire began, "All right, Adam, go ahead and tell us when the last time was that you saw your wife and what you did until you got the call from the school telling you she hadn't picked up your daughter."

"Ann left the house around 7:30 yesterday morning. That's the last time I saw her. I went to work and spent the day with Marcus Williams working on the Devon Jackson case." There was an edge to his voice when he said, "And you can check that out with Marcus."

"We will," Manson said, "The faster we get you cleared, the quicker we can figure out what happened to your wife."

"Sorry if I snapped at you, Matt. I know how it works. Go ahead."

"That's all right. Can you think of anyone that would have seen or heard from Ann in the morning?"

"I know she stops every morning at the Starbucks on Savannah Highway. They know her there and ought to be able to confirm whether or not she stopped by yesterday. Plus, she always uses her credit card, so you can run a check on the card."

"Good, we'll follow up on that. How about at her office? Does anyone work with her, or is there anyone else who might have seen her that morning?"

"Ann's a one-woman office, but there's a doctor that works in the other half of the building. She's a psychiatrist. Her name is Kate Shaw. Their offices have separate entrances, but she might have seen her."

"We're gonna need her phone number." Adam had Dr. Shaw's number in his cell and gave it to Manson. "Now, you mentioned that accountant that stopped at Ann's office yesterday afternoon. I'll need his name and phone number." Like Shaw, Adam had Bennett's number in his phone and passed it on.

Finally, Manson stood and said, "I need your wife's office address and key. We're also going to want to check out her office and home computers. We need to get out there and tape it up. Nobody gets in without our approval. That means you, too. If anything did happen, we need to preserve the place. It's no secret you're on the Blood's shit list for taking out Salazar. We'll talk to Merchant, but I'm sure he's already got his street people cranking up the pressure on them."

They spent another ten minutes or so reviewing what else they needed to do. As the meeting was breaking up, Claire

Charles pulled Adam aside. "We got this, Adam. Whatever it takes."

"I know, Claire. Thanks. Just make sure you keep me in the loop."

Back in the bullpen, Marcus was on the phone. "Gotta go, babe. He's here. I'll call you later."

Adam slid behind his desk but said nothing.

"Any word?"

"No. Chief's putting Charles Manson on it."

Marcus sounded a bit surprised when he said, "Chief gave this to Homicide already?"

Charleston's Homicide Department consisted of eight detectives that operated out of what everyone referred to as "The Kennels." The guys in Homicide were known as the "pit bulls," because of their dogged persistence pursuing their investigations. Years ago, someone had hung a framed picture of a pit bull on the wall next to the stairs leading out of the Kennels. Homicide detectives never left the Kennels without patting the picture for good luck. It looked like there was a chance that someone might have attacked one of their own, and now the leashes were coming off.

Marcus saw the dark bags under Adam's eyes—possum eyes. "Did you get any sleep?"

Adam's answer was a curt. "What'd you think?"

"Right. Listen, they just brought Jackson over. Let me deal with him. Why don't you go home and get some rest?"

"Rest?" Adam said, sarcasm evident. "I don't think so. You heard what Jackson said yesterday. The Bloods know I shot Salazar, and it doesn't take a genius to figure out who might have taken Ann. Let's go."

Devon Jackson was back in Room One, his left hand cuffed to a metal chair. As soon as Adam entered the room, he smiled at Jackson and said, "Happy birthday, asshole. I heard you just turned eighteen. Guess you're a big boy now."

Devon just glared at Stone, not knowing what to make of the comment.

"Damn, Detective Stone," Marcus added. "You're right. Our boy's an adult now. Ten grams of heroin. If my memory's right, Devon just bought himself up to ten years in one of our state's fine prisons."

Jackson remained quiet. He knew what was coming next.

Marcus didn't waste any time. "Who supplies the Bloods?"

Devon had run out of luck. He'd always told his crew that life was like a crap shoot: "Don't roll the dice, if you can't pay the price." But he also knew the life he'd chosen would eventually roll him a seven.

He shook his head. "No way. I talk, I'm history, man."

Stone put both hands on the table and leaned in close—inches from Devon's face. "You're already history to me, you punk-ass prick. Who has my wife?"

An almost imperceptible smirk registered on Devon's face. "Don't know what you're talking about, detective."

An instant later, Adam had a handful of Devon's dreadlocks and slammed his face into the metal table.

Marcus was on him in a second, pushing him against the wall. "Back off, partner. We can't blow this one."

"All right," Stone seethed, eyes glued on Jackson. "I'm all right."

Still holding him back, Marcus shot a look at the two-way mirror and shook his head—a clear signal to ditch the videotape of what had just happened. He let go of Adam's shirt. "Be cool now. Be cool."

Jackson was holding his head—his eyes shooting hollow point bullets at Stone. "I want a damn lawyer."

It didn't take long before word got back to Chief Taylor, who sent Adam home for the rest of the day. "I see that shit again, Stone, and you're taking a vacation. Understood?"

"Yes, sir. I'm sorry. It won't happen again."

~~~~

It wasn't even noon yet, and Adam was wound tight when he left the station. His wife was missing, and everything pointed to the Bloods. He felt responsible. He'd taken out Cedric Salazar, and this might be payback. He'd promised Chief Taylor he'd stay out of the way, but no way was that happening. He took the Crosstown to I-26 and headed for North Charleston.

Most street cops and detectives develop special contacts within the local criminal community. This is especially true for officers working vice. Adam had developed his own crew of so-called "snitches" over the past two decades. The department brass knew about most of them, but Adam kept the identity of a few in his back pocket. The ones he kept to himself were fairly well placed in their respective criminal organizations, and
~~~~

their lives would be in danger if their relationship with Stone were ever discovered.

While there are several ways to "turn" someone, it usually begins by catching the perp committing a crime. As long as the crime wasn't something like terrorism or murder, a detective could let it slide with the understanding that there would be an ongoing *quid pro quo*. The criminals knew that from that time forward, the cop owned them.

Stone had an impressive stable of bookies, hookers, bagmen, and other snitches, one of whom was a member of the Bloods named Jayden King. King looked like Bruno Mars, but that's where the resemblance ended. He was like one of those sharks on the Discovery Channel's *Shark Week*—always circling and opportunistic. Adam had busted him on a felony drug charge. He had two priors, which meant he was facing some serious time if convicted. Three strikes and you're out. Jayden had little choice but to roll—but Adam knew there was always the chance he could roll right back.

Jayden hung around the BP station on the corner of Ashley Phosphate and Stull Road—a tough area of North Charleston known for drugs and prostitution—an area Adam knew well. He slowed the Charger as he approached the BP. He rolled down his window and let his left arm hang out. As soon as Jayden saw him, Adam nonchalantly tapped the car door once—a signal he wanted to meet. Their preset meeting place was at the far end of the parking lot outside Dillard's Department Store at Citadel Mall.

Adam knew dying shopping malls were scattered across the country, but he couldn't help but mourn the glory days of the Citadel Mall as he navigated its deserted parking lot. The onslaught of the internet and the explosion of online shopping had once again taken their toll. He was just a kid when Citadel Mall opened in 1981 to packed parking lots and stores over-flowing with shoppers. But now the huge parking lots around the mall were virtually empty, and the inside of the mall itself resembled a ghost town. It wouldn't be long before the whole place was out of business.

Adam had been waiting a half hour when a beat-up Chevy Impala pulled alongside him, its bass thumping the windows of his Charger. Jayden King got out and slid into the front seat next to Adam.

"What is it now, Stone? I get made with you, and I'm fucked."

"I'll make sure to add that to my list of things I don't give a shit about."

"Just tell me what the fuck you want."

Adam shook his head. "Language, Jayden. Haven't I told you about using bad words? It's very unbecoming. Now, shut the hell up and listen. Did your people take my wife? You lie to me, and I'll let your Bloods pals know you and I are good buddies."

King knew he'd be killed if it was discovered that he'd been snitching for Stone. "I don't know for sure, but I don't think so." The department had come down like a sledge-hammer on the Bloods—it was crushing their business. Word was the Bloods wouldn't do anything to piss off the cops, at least until things settled down.

"All right," Adam said. "Give me a heads up if anything changes, or I'll be paying you another visit. Do we understand each other?"

"Yeah," King answered. "That all?"

"Sure, Jayden. Have yourself a nice day."

Adam still wasn't convinced the Bloods hadn't taken Ann, but King's information had always been solid. Adam left the parking lot still trying to make sense of everything. Someone might have taken Ann, and if it wasn't the Bloods, then who? Maybe one of her patients. He'd always been concerned that Ann dealt with people that could be unpredictable due to their mental health issues. She tried to downplay it, but Adam knew it was something she had to consider in her practice.

He decided to take another look at Ann's office. He'd only spent a few minutes there yesterday, and there was a good chance he might have missed something. He'd given Ann's office key to Charles Manson but remembered she'd hid a spare one under a rock behind the stairs leading up to her office. Once inside, he found an empty Starbucks cup in the waste-basket next to her desk. Maybe she did stop at Starbucks yesterday morning. But maybe it was left there from the day before. He checked for messages on Ann's answering machine. The accountant, Bennett, had called twice, first at 3:10 and then again at 3:15. There was one at 5:35 from Jenny Black at Charleston Collegiate and the rest were the several calls he and Tracy had made Thursday evening and Friday morning.

Knowing Charles Manson would probably be there shortly, he left the office, locking the door behind him. He was approaching the ramp leading to Ashley River Memorial Bridge when his cell vibrated. It was Chief Taylor.

"Yes, sir?"

"Adam, where are you now?"

He didn't want Taylor to know he was doing his own investigating—exactly what he'd just told the Chief he wouldn't do. "Just thinking about getting something to eat. Why? What's up?"

Chief Taylor had made calls like this before and knew there was no easy way out. The line was silent for a few seconds before he said, "We found Ann. Adam, I don't know how to say this … she's dead."

Adam closed his eyes. He couldn't move—couldn't breathe. His mind plummeted to the edge of darkness. He managed to pull the Charger to the side of the road. "Where?"

"Adam, are you all right to make it back to the station?"

"Where is she?"

"Come back to the station. We're all here for you."

Adam hung up. His breathing quickened. There was a ringing in his ear. Then it started—a low guttural sound rising from deep within. It grew louder as he slammed down on the accelerator and the Charger fishtailed back on to the road. He could barely keep control of the car, as he raced across the bridge toward downtown—his hands at ten and two on the steering wheel—his speed approaching eighty. The ringing in his ears hadn't stopped when he slammed on the brakes and skidded to a stop in front of Lockwood. He was out of the car running to the station when Marcus grabbed him. He tried to push away but was no match for Marcus. Finally, Adam's body went limp, and they made their way up the steps and into the station together.

Taylor and Merchant were waiting inside the door and helped Stone down the hallway and into the chief's office. Merchant shut the door as Adam slumped into a chair. Marcus took the seat next to him—his eyes never leaving his friend.

A strange stillness came over Stone. The ringing was gone. His eyes closed and his breathing slowed. He was spent but emotionally under control. Surreal. His voice was surprisingly placid. "Tell me what happened."

"God Adam, we're so sorry."

"Tell me what happened," Adam calmly repeated.

It was Marcus who spoke, "The station got an anonymous call about an hour ago. We tried to trace it, but it was made from a burner. Officers followed up and found Ann at a small boat landing in McClellanville."

"What happened to her?"

"Charles and Manson are out there now, and CSI is on their way," Taylor said.

"What happened to her?" Adam repeated and turned toward Marcus. "I'm okay, but I need to know."

Marcus hesitated, then lowered his voice. "Throat was cut. It would have been quick."

Adam remained unusually calm. "I want to see her."

"Forensic techs will be working the scene," Taylor said. "You'll eventually need to identify. In the meantime, whatever you need."

"I need to leave," Adam said. "I've got to tell Ann's mom and Piper before … you know, before." It was clear that word of Ann's murder would soon hit the airwaves and internet.

Marcus walked out with Adam. "You want me to come with you?"

"No. I need to do this myself."

Without another word, the two men hugged. Marcus whispered, "Lean on me, brother. You know I'm always here. We'll get the scum that did this. You have my word."

~~~~

Adam left Lockwood and headed across the connector to Tracy's house. Piper was still in school and wouldn't need to be picked up until later that afternoon. Since a massive coronary had taken Tracy's husband five years ago, her life had revolved around her daughter and granddaughter. Adam had just experienced his own life shattering, and now he was about to bring that same world-annihilating news to his wife's mother. It was almost more than he could bear, but he knew that for both her sake and Piper's, he was going to have to find the strength to face the unimaginable with them.

Adam pulled into the driveway and sat there a few minutes, trying to reign in his emotions. He was about to tell Tracy her daughter was dead. He was almost to the front door
~~~~

when it opened. Tracy started to speak, but then she saw Adam's face, his moist, bloodshot eyes, and she knew.

"Tracy," he whispered.

She held onto the door and slowly shook her head back and forth. Her eyes closed and her legs gave. Adam caught her and held her up. "They found her," he somehow managed to say. "I'm sorry. We lost her. She's dead."

"My baby. Oh God, my baby. No!" she screamed and pounded Adam's chest.

He continued to hold her until all the strength poured out of her. She began to sob as he half-walked, half-carried her to the living room couch—her tears flowing freely.

Eventually, Adam let her go and she gazed up at him, her eyes the saddest thing he'd ever seen. "What happened?"

"We don't know yet. They found her in McClellanville this morning. The police and detectives are trying to figure out what happened. Tracy, Piper doesn't know."

"Oh, God. Piper."

"I was going to pick her up early, but I figure she may as well have a few more normal hours before she knows what happened. I'll pick her up in about an hour. Can you come stay with us for a while? This is going to be hell for all of us, and we need to be together. Will you do that?"

"Yes, of course. I know I don't want to be alone and … poor Piper." The tears returned. "God, I don't even know where to begin."

~~~~
~~~~

Adam was cued up in the car line at Charleston Collegiate waiting to pick up Piper. His mind raced. How do you tell a twelve-year-old she'll never see her mother again? How do you tell her she'll never share her first kiss, her first broken heart, her first true love—and the myriad other things that make up a life shared between a mother and daughter? He was still wrestling with what to say when the passenger door opened, and Piper slid in.

"Hi, Dad."

"Hi, baby."

"Did Mom get home?"

"No."

Adam pulled into a small park about a quarter of a mile from Piper's school. He parked and shut off the engine.

"Why are we stopping?"

"Let's take a walk."

They got out, and Adam led her to a metal bench just off the parking area. "Sit down, sweetheart."

She began to panic. "Dad. What's going on … did something happen to Mom?"

"Piper, something's happened. I just want you to know that Granny and I will always be here for you." He took her hand and continued. "Mom's gone to heaven."

"I don't understand. What?"

There was nothing more Adam could say. "I'm sorry, honey. Mom died."

Piper couldn't say anything—still trying to process the word *died*.

Adam pulled her close. She looked up at him, her lips starting to quiver. "Why?" was all she said, and then she began to cry.

~~~~

They sat there holding each other for some time before eventually returning to the car. Adam continued to hold Piper's hand as he drove home. It was clear she still hadn't completely understood or accepted what had happened to her mother. The drive to their house took what seemed like a lifetime.

Tracy and Max were waiting by the front door when Adam pulled in. Piper ran to her. They hugged and Tracy whispered, "Oh, baby. My sweet child. My sweet, sweet child."

The three of them sat together in the living room—Adam and Tracy dealing with their own emotions but doing what they could to console Piper. "We all need to stay strong," Tracy finally said. "Your mom would want that, honey."

News of the murder was already churning on the internet, and there was no doubt television and radio coverage wouldn't be far behind. By 5:00 that evening, the news of the murder of the wife of a Charleston detective had caught fire on the evening news. All three local news channels had reporters broadcasting from the McClellanville boat landing. It didn't take long before Adam's phone started buzzing. After receiving calls from Kate Shaw and several family friends, he felt drained. He wasn't ready to face the outside world, and he set his phone on
~~~~

'Do Not Disturb.' He knew that the most important thing right now was being there for his daughter.

Eventually, Tracy made dinner, even though it was unlikely anyone would touch a bite. Max jumped on the couch and laid his head on Piper's lap. Emotionally spent, Adam sat with Piper, each lost in their own thoughts. The whole thing felt like some kind of dream—more like a nightmare. They ate in silence, hardly touching their food.

After dinner, Tracy took Piper to her room and stayed with her until she finally fell asleep—Max curled up next to her. Once Tracy was sure Piper was asleep, she joined Adam in the living room. He was seated with his head down nursing a cup of coffee—the silenced television playing in the background showing a reporter broadcasting from in front of the Lockwood Police Station.

"Why did this happen, Adam?"

"I don't know. I just don't know. Chief's got the whole department working on it. But the important thing is to stay strong for Piper. I'll need to be gone at times over the next few days, and you know the media will continue to be all over this. You're going to need to be there for her. Can you do that?"

The answer was obvious. She didn't need to respond. She just patted his arm and went off wearily to her room to look for answers she knew she wouldn't find.

He'd hardly slept in two days, and the rollercoaster he'd ridden left him emotionally and physically drained. His eyes felt like two burnt out pieces of coal. The demands of the day had also hit Tracy hard, and they both knew they would need sleep to deal with what was to come. He checked his phone and was somewhat surprised to discover that Kate Shaw had left three more messages. He made another call to Lockwood. Nothing new. Adam still found it difficult to fall asleep, and it was well after midnight before he finally succumbed.

# CHAPTER THREE

### Saturday, March 3

A WISP OF morning slipped through his bedroom window, carving out shadows and sending slivers of soft light across the walls. Dust motes floated in the still air. He glanced to his left and noticed his daughter fast asleep next to him. Not wanting to be alone, she'd obviously come into his room sometime during the night. Max, eyes closed, was curled up at the foot of the bed. Adam got up, careful not to wake them, and slipped on his bathrobe. He left the bedroom, quietly easing the door shut behind him.

Tracy sat at the kitchen table, her complexion pale and deep lines on her face evident. She looked older than she had the previous day.

Adam poured a cup of coffee and sat with her. "I'm going to have to leave shortly."

Her gaze focused on the middle distance. It was a few seconds before she crawled out of her mind and responded. "Sorry, dear, I didn't get much sleep last night. You go ahead and do what you need to do. We'll be okay."

"Thanks, I'll be back as soon as I can. See how Piper feels, but it might be good to get her out. I wouldn't be surprised if reporters show up at the house. I'll leave you one of my credit cards. If she's up to it, maybe you two can go to Dairy Queen or take a hike on the Greenway. You know, keep her busy as much as you can."

"Okay," Tracy said, somewhat snapping out of her daze. "We can also take Max to the dog park. We'll stay busy." There was a huge four-acre dog park complete with a small lake inside the James Island County Park. Adam and Piper made a practice of taking Max there several times a week.

~~~~

It was Saturday morning, and the bullpen was unusually active—many detectives had come in on their day off to help with the Stone killing. A stack of pink messages stared at him from his desk. He ignored the messages and headed upstairs to the Kennels.
~~~~

Claire Charles was at her desk on the phone. She noticed Adam and pointed to the seat next to her. A moment later, she hung up and said, "That was Matt. He's on his way in. How are you holding up?"

Adam ignored the question and said, "What have you got so far?"

"The crime scene guys finished up at the boat landing. They did their thing—dusted for prints, made some footprint casts of the area. There were a lot of tire tracks, so it'll be tough to identify the type of tire on the vehicle used. They're still processing what they got. We'll have to wait for DNA results. The coroner said the knife used had a serrated blade, most likely a tactical one similar to the Ka-Bar knives used by the army." Claire paused for a moment and said, "Adam, you sure you want to hear this?"

"Yeah. Go ahead."

It was clear Clair was uncomfortable. "All right, it looked like whoever did this knew what they were doing. The jugular was slit. That means she would have been unconscious within seconds and gone within minutes. Apparently, the boat landing isn't used that much, so it's unlikely anyone would have seen anything. Officers canvassed the area but didn't find anyone who might have seen what happened. Plus, the coroner said it would have happened in the middle of the night."

Claire paused. "Sorry, Adam, but you know I gotta ask. I'm assuming you were at home asleep last night. Can anyone vouch for you?"

"Just Ann's mother and my daughter."

"I'm sorry, but it doesn't seem we've got much to go on yet. We stopped by and taped up Ann's office yesterday. Believe it or not, a few reporters had already stopped by her building. I'm meeting Matt and forensics there shortly. We'll process the office and pick up her home computer when we're finished.

"Listen, Claire, I know where Ann keeps her patient information and other stuff. I can meet you there."

"Sorry, no can do. You heard the chief. We'll call you if we've got any questions. When we're done, we'll swing by your house to get the computer. I promise we'll update you then."

"All right, the keys to her filing cabinets are in her desk attached to a keychain labeled *PF*. But don't expect to get anything off her home computer. She never uses it for her practice."

"Maybe not, but we still need to check it out. Also, there's a chance whoever did this might be someone your investigations or testimony put in jail or sent to prison. Marcus told us Devon Jackson threatened you yesterday during his interrogation. And we know your history with the Bloods. Can you think of anyone else we need to be aware of?"

"Jesus, Claire, I've been doing this for almost twenty years. I've put hundreds of criminals in prison. You need to focus on the Bloods."

"I know that. But think about it and let us know about anyone else that's actually threatened you."

"All right. But have you followed up on the Bloods?"

"Not yet, but Merchant's already started on that. He's got the department calling in markers and canvasing the usual suspects. They'll rattle some cages and see what shakes out. You worked vice. You know the drill. I promise we'll let you know what we find."

Adam nodded at a manila folder on the side of Claire's desk holding what looked like photographs. He pointed to the folder. "Did you take those?"

She quickly slid her hand over the folder. "I don't think you need to see those. We'll deal with them."

Adam stared at the folder for a few seconds, then shifted his gaze back to Claire. "I need to see them."

Her hand remained on the folder of photos. "No, Adam, you don't. Trust me."

Adam said nothing—his stare still focused on her.

Finally, Claire said, "Shit," and gave Adam the folder.

It contained ten 8" X 10" glossy colored photos of the crime scene—several showing Ann. The shots were gruesome—some as bad or worse than the horrific images that had been floating to the surface of his mind since Ann disappeared.

Adam studied each photo, then slid them back in the folder. "Excuse me," he said, and walked to the men's room. He opened one of the stalls and dropped to his knees. He remained there for a few moments fighting the urge to vomit. Finally, he rose, went to the sink, rinsed his mouth, and splashed water on his face. Using paper towels, he dried his face and hands and left the restroom.

When Adam returned to Claire's desk, the folder was gone.

"Are you all right?"

"Yeah. I just gotta go." He turned wearily knowing he needed to formally identify Ann's body.

"Wait, there's something else," Claire said.

Adam turned back and sat.

"The news channels are hot and heavy on the story, and what I'm going to tell you has to stay on the down low. Only Matt, Taylor, Merchant, and the crime scene guys know about it."

In high-profile cases, police often keep a few crime scene details secret during their investigation. If a suspect knows nonpublic information about a crime, it increases the likelihood that they either committed it or, at least, might know who did. It also helps police rule out the possibility that a suspect might be confessing to a crime they didn't commit. Highly public murder cases tend to bring out the crazies.

Adam leaned forward, "Go ahead."

"First, whoever did this, took a section of Ann's hair." She paused, then continued, "And he left something. It was a votive candle. We think it was burning in her hands when the killer left."

"What the hell does that mean?"

"We're not exactly sure. These things are also called prayer candles, and they're often burned to indicate a sacrifice, or a prayer to the dead."

Adam thought for a moment. "Did you run it through NCIC?" NCIC is the acronym for the National Crime Information Center. It had been acting as a clearing house for information on criminal activity since the FBI founded it in 1967.

"We did. Filtered the database using keywords like *candle*, *prayer*, and *religious*. Got a few hits where a candle was left at a murder scene, but they were mostly old cases. Some solved, but most totally cold. As far as we can tell, the persons associated with the solved cases are all either still in prison or dead. And none of the cold cases happened in the Charleston area."

"So, what does that tell us?" The question was more for himself than Claire. "If Ann's murder has a religious aspect to it, we still can't rule out the Bloods. Sounds strange, but most of them have some sort of a religious background. We see a lot of them with tatts of a cross, or they'll wear one around their neck. Any prints on the candle?"

"No. Wiped clean. And there's no way we can trace it. You're probably right about the Bloods, but we also need to interview Ann's patients. Hell, she was dealing with people with mental and emotional problems every day."

"You're right. She's mentioned that. She even attended a seminar on how to identify and deal with patients that might pose a threat."

Claire quickly added, "There's always the possibility we missed something on the NCIC. Like I said, none of the cold cases was around Charleston, but we can't rule out a connection. The candle could be how this asshole signs his kills, and he probably took a lock of Ann's hair as a memento or trophy to prolong the fantasy of the kill."

"I suppose it could have been a robbery gone bad or some random act," Adam said, "but I don't buy that. Too many things don't make sense. There's no evidence of a break-in, and Ann never made her three o'clock meeting with the accountant. She was probably taken before that. The coroner said it could have been up to twelve hours from the time Ann disappeared to when she was killed. Plus, whoever did it, there's the lock of her hair and the burning candle. It seems too much like some ritual thing."

Claire said something, but Adam didn't hear her. All he could think of was the killer holding a lock of Ann's hair.

~~~~

Adam left the station knowing the photos he'd seen of Ann and the crime scene were only a precursor of what was to come next. A short time later, he turned into the county morgue. The drive was a blur. He couldn't even guess the number of times he'd been there over his twenty years on the force. But this time everything was different—the smells, the sights, the sounds were more invasive—more stark and real. Neil Westbrook, one of the medical examiners, met him at the door. "I'm sorry seeing you under these circumstances, Adam. Are you ready for this?"

"Let's just do it." He knew he'd never be ready for what he was about to see.
~~~~

Westbrook led Adam down a hall and through a metal door into a brightly lit room. There was a steady hum from the fluorescent lights, and the air was noticeably cooler and had a pungent antiseptic smell to it. Both the floor and walls were made of off-white porcelain tile. The room contained several stainless-steel sinks, cabinets, and tables. Another heavy metal door on the far wall led to a large refrigerated room in which the bagged and tagged bodies were kept. There were two autopsy stations—the one on the right had a body covered with a light blue tarp.

Westbrook pointed. "Ann's over here."

He gently pulled the tarp down only enough to show Ann's face—taking care to keep her lacerated throat covered. It was clear that a portion of Ann's hair was missing.

Adam closed his eyes and looked away. "Yes," he said.

Westbrook quickly covered Ann's face. "Thank you." He took Adam's elbow and gently led him from the room.

After signing the Death Certificate, they shook hands. "Sorry, Adam, but it had to be done."

"I understand. When will you release the body?"

"I should finish up tonight or tomorrow morning. Which funeral home are you using? I'll make the transportation arrangements."

"McAlister-Smith on Folly Road. I'm on my way there now."

<p style="text-align:center">~~~~</p>

The next few hours were taken up making arrangements at the funeral home and cemetery. The graveside service would be limited to family and a few close friends. The murder was still garnering widespread coverage, and arrangements were made to keep the news media from the gravesite. A catered reception at the Citadel Alumni Center would follow the funeral service. This would give the department and other friends of the family an opportunity to pay their respects. The department would cover the cost of the reception. Adam checked in several times with Tracy who was doing her best to keep Piper occupied as much as possible.

He had just left the funeral home when he received a call from Claire Charles. "Adam, we're at Ann's office, and we can't find her computer or iPad."

"They both should be on her desk in her office. She never brings either of them home."

"Well," Claire continued, "we checked everywhere, and neither of them are here. Plus, the patient files we found in her filing cabinets only have basic contact and billing information. We can't find any of the notes she takes when she's with her patients. Are we missing something?"

Adam couldn't believe he'd missed the fact that Ann's office computer was gone but said nothing about it.

"She doesn't have any written notes. She only uses the iPad when she's with a patient. Everything's electronic now. Every week or so, she transfers the stuff from the iPad to individual patient folders on her office computer. The iPad should be there. I told you she never brings them home."

"Well, it's not here. Is there any other place she'd keep that information?"

"No, not as far as I know."

"How about the Cloud?" Claire persisted. "Does she use it?"

"No. Doesn't trust it. She said medical records are the number one target for criminal hackers. But she does back up her files on flash drives."

"Where would they be?"

"In her desk. Top drawer on the left, if I remember correctly."

"Hang on," Claire said. A moment later she was back on the line. "They're not there. I checked all the drawers." It was becoming clear that whoever killed Ann took her computer along with the iPad and flash drives.

"If it's not the Bloods, it could have been one of her patients," Adam offered. "I can't think of anyone else that would do something like this."

"Yeah, that's still our best guess," Claire replied, "Wait a minute. Why the hell would the Bloods care about her patient records? Doesn't make any sense. Gotta be one of her patients."

"You're probably right. But I'm not ready to pass on the Bloods. I killed Cedric. That's one hell of a motive."

"Right," Claire said. "Hang on, Matt wants to talk to you."

A few seconds later, Matt was on the line. "I wanted to let you know we did check with the Starbucks you said Ann stops at. They were pretty sure she stopped by Thursday morning.

We checked her credit card, and it did show a Starbuck's charge that morning of $14.00."

"Well, at least we know she got to her office," Adam said.

"There's something else. You said Ann's only appointment that day was with the accountant, right?"

"Yeah, that's the only one I saw on her calendar. I talked to him last night, and he told me that when he got to her office it was locked and no one was there. He said he called Ann's cell and office number. She didn't answer."

"How well do you know this guy," Matt asked.

"Pretty well, I guess. Ann was working at the VA when we got married but left a few years later when we had Piper. Money got pretty tight back then, plus Ann was getting a little antsy, so we decided it was time for her to get back to work. Ann knew Kate Shaw from when she worked at the VA, and Kate convinced her to start her own practice. She hooked her up with Bennett, and he helped Ann get her practice started. He's done both Ann's business and our personal taxes for the past ten years or so. Ann knows him better than I do. He lives in Mt. Pleasant, so I don't see him all that much."

"We'll be talking to him and Dr. Shaw as soon as the techs finish up here. The Bennett guy was the only appointment your wife had scheduled that day. He's a prime suspect as far as we're concerned, and we don't want you talking to him or Dr. Shaw, okay? If they call, keep it basic, accept their condolences and be done with it."

Adam saw a way to get more directly involved and said, "Wait a second, I've got an idea. Just hear me out, okay? We've got to assume both Bennett and Shaw have seen news reports about the murder. Bennett was at her office that afternoon and must know he's gonna be a prime suspect. He might shut down when you two show up. He knows me, so let me follow up with him on Monday. I can use the excuse that I want him to handle probate and whatever other filings there might be. Actually, it makes sense he'd be the one I'd pick anyway. He knows our financial information and Ann's business records. He'll trust me more than two detectives he's never met. It's already three o'clock, and my bank's closed. Ann's will and other financial stuff is in our safety deposit box, and I'll tell him I can get the documents and drop them off Monday."

"I don't think so," Matt said, "You heard the chief."

"I know, but remember he also said it was up to you guys to use me if you wanted to. Come on, I can do this. You know I won't screw it up."

"Hang on," Matt said. A moment later, he was back on the phone. "All right, Adam, you're in but keep it simple. Don't spook him. And call us as soon as you finish."

"Thanks, Matt. I appreciate that."

As soon as Adam hung up, he called Bennett. "Hello, Bill. It's Adam Stone."

"Lord in heaven. I'm so sorry, Adam. I heard about Ann. May God have mercy on her soul."

Adam let the comment pass. "I hope I'm not interrupting anything."

"No, not at all. I'm still at church. I spend Saturdays here helping out with things. What can I do to help?"

"Actually, that's why I'm calling, Bill. I'd like you to handle probate and whatever other financial stuff that needs to be done."

"Of course."

"I'm going to get Ann's will and the other paperwork you'll need from the bank Monday morning. Have you got time to meet Monday?"

"I'll make time, Adam. Whatever works for you?"

"How about around 11:00? I'll come by your office."

"That works. I still can't believe something like this could happen, but God works in mysterious ways."

Adam bit his tongue and simply said, "I'll see you Monday morning."

~~~~

Tracy and Piper were still out when Charles Manson met Adam at the house to pick up Ann's computer. They had just left, and Adam was having a cup of coffee in the kitchen when Tracy entered with an arm full of groceries. She was followed by Piper who went straight to her bedroom. Tracy frowned, turned to Adam, and said, "There's more in the car."

"How did Piper do today?"

"We had a tough time but got through it. When we left this morning, a news truck was outside of the house. We talked a lot, and she's doing the best she can. I told her that when Paul had his heart attack and passed away, I put all my thoughts and feelings in the form of a letter to him. It helped. That's what
~~~~

she's doing now; writing a letter to Ann. Adam, I don't know how much more of this I can take."

"I know." He felt helpless. "Can I help with dinner?"

"No. Why don't you just get the groceries and take Max for a walk? I'll take care of dinner." She finally managed a smile. "I seem to remember your expertise in the kitchen has always been centered around the microwave."

They had a quiet dinner with Piper excusing herself early and returning to her room. Once Piper left, Tracy wanted to know what Adam had learned and if the police had discovered any new evidence that would help explained what happened. He did what he could to reassure her but made no mention of his visit to the morgue or his dealings with the Bloods.

Even though Piper was twelve and an excellent reader, she'd asked Tracy if they could read together that evening. Tracy headed off to Piper's bedroom, and Adam grabbed Max's leash and took him out for his nightly walk. He was thinking about what else could be done to move the investigation forward and the myriad of other things that needed to be done in the next few days when he noticed an older black Camaro parked a few houses down from his own. It seemed out of place—cut low to the ground with tinted windows and custom rims. Adam memorized the plate number, and once he got back inside, wrote it down. When he returned to the front porch, the Camaro was gone.

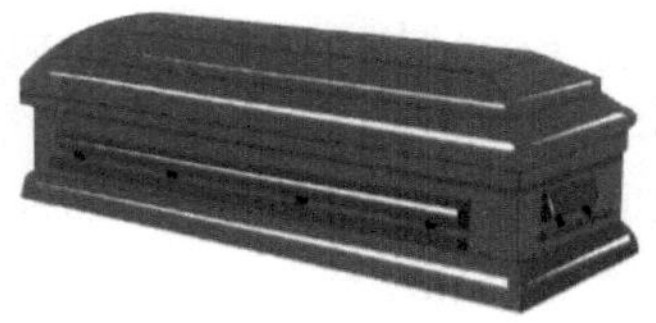

# **CHAPTER FOUR**

Sunday, March 4

KNOWING PIPER WOULD be sleeping in, Adam left for Lockwood first thing Sunday morning. He also knew Charles Manson would be working 24/7, especially in the early stages, when the chances of solving the murder plummeted with each passing hour. This was the third day since Ann had been killed, and the clock was ticking.

He made a quick stop at his desk then headed upstairs. With the exception of Claire Charles, the room was empty.

"Where's Matt?"

Claire made a vague motion towards the small room down the hall. "The Bunkhouse, getting a little sleep. We've been at it." The Bunkhouse is a small room on the second floor that detectives used to catch a few hours of sleep while working a case. Adam pulled up a chair and settled his gaze on Claire. "Don't pull any punches. I need to know."

"Okay. A couple of things. We got the autopsy report early this morning. Lab analysis showed traces of propofol in Ann's blood. Looks like whoever did this used the drug to keep her unconscious for several hours. Propofol is the same drug they say killed Michael Jackson. Pretty potent stuff. It's not easy to get, but since it showed up in Jackson's autopsy, people know to look for it and, if they have enough money, they can usually find it. Hell, you can find just about anything on the street. The autopsy indicated the cause of death was exsanguination and noted that Ann was probably unconscious when she died."

Adam paused a few seconds. The question had been on his mind. "Was Ann … was she raped?"

"No, there's no evidence of any of that. Plus, she was fully clothed when the officer found her."

"There's something I don't understand," Adam said. "Ann's Fiat wasn't in the lot at her office when I stopped by Thursday afternoon. And it wasn't out at the boat landing in McClellanville, either. Where is it?"

"We found it behind the ice cream shop at the corner of Wesley Drive and Savannah Highway. The owner called it in yesterday. He said it had been there for a few days. There's a car detailing business behind the guy's shop, and he assumed that's why it was there. The shop's only about a half mile from

Ann's office, so we figure whoever got her moved the Fiat there."

"What about security cameras? They gotta show when it was dropped off."

"No, the owner has cameras inside and at the front of his building but not in the rear of it."

"That was smart," Adam said, sarcastically. "Anyway, did Westbrook estimate the time of death?" Adam felt strange using the phrase *time of death* when talking about Ann. It felt too procedural, too callous.

"Yeah. He put it at somewhere between two and five Friday morning."

All Adam could think about was all those hours Ann might have been with whoever took her. He knew she was probably abducted before 3:00 Thursday afternoon, and that meant it could have been up to twelve hours.

He tried to shake that thought out of his mind and asked, "What else?"

"We'll check the pharmacies for propofol prescriptions even though that's not likely to turn up anything. Also, Ann's building doesn't have any security cameras. We had officers canvass the area to see if anyone noticed anything—no luck with that."

"You said you were going to interview Kate Shaw and Bill Bennett. What did you learn? I know Bennett said he never saw Ann. I also phoned Kate Shaw the same night Ann went missing, and she said she never saw her that day. Did you get anything else out of either of them?"

"We did talk to both of them. The accountant, Bennett, said he was in his office all Thursday morning, but left around noon to see two of his clients about their tax returns. His secretary backed him up on that, and the two clients confirmed they met with Bennett early that afternoon. Like he told you, when he went there for their 3:00 appointment, she wasn't there."

"How about Dr. Shaw?"

"She told us she was with patients all day and didn't see Ann at all. She wasn't very cooperative when we asked for the names and phone numbers of those patients. Patient confidentiality. A little 'good cop, bad cop,' and a promise the information would stay inside the department finally got her to agree. Plus, the threat of a subpoena didn't hurt. We'll follow up with both of them, but even if we confirm what they told us, there's holes in each of their alibies. We're going to bring them into the station and follow up as soon as we finish confirming what they told us."

Adam removed the note with the Camaro's plate number. "Run that."

Claire entered the plate number in South Carolina's Law Enforcement Information Network (LEIN) database. The result appeared immediately. She shifted the computer screen so Adam could see the results. The screen identified the vehicle to be a 2003 Camaro SS. It also showed the vehicle identification number (VIN), plate expiration date, and any violations, suspensions, or outstanding warrants issued on the registered owner.

"Son of a bitch," Adam said. The Camaro was registered to a Vincent Salazar.

Claire asked, "Where'd you get that plate number?"

"That Camaro was sitting outside my house last night. Vincent is Cedric Salazar's little brother. I need to get this to Merchant and see what vice knows about him."

Claire Charles shook her head. "No, Adam, you need to leave that kind of thing to us. You heard the chief—he doesn't want you near this stuff."

"Well, it looks like I'm fucking near it now!" Adam quickly caught himself. "Sorry Claire. You're right. It's just that I'm going to bury my wife on Wednesday, and now I gotta deal with this shit."

Claire put her hand on Adam's shoulder. "I hear you. I'll get all this to Merchant and the chief and let you know. In the meantime, we should probably have officers watching your house."

Adam shook his head. "Thanks, but no way is that happening. I don't want my daughter or Ann's mother seeing a bunch of police officers sitting outside the house and thinking they're in a war zone. I'll be with them, and if I can't, I'd rather have Marcus there. He's like family."

"That's up to the chief, but I think he'll buy it."

"Thanks. Tell Matt I appreciate everything you guys are doing. I need to get back home before my daughter wakes up. Let me know if you get anything else from Shaw or Bennett."

"You got it, and we'll talk to Taylor and Merchant about Vincent Salazar."

# CHAPTER FIVE

Monday, March 5

ADAM WAS UP Monday morning, and after retrieving what he needed from his bank, he made the thirty-minute drive across the Ravenel Bridge to Bill Bennett's Mt. Pleasant office.

His Coleman Boulevard office was relatively small but pleasant. After receiving condolences from Bennett's receptionist and assistant, Bill led Adam into his office. It was also small, but immaculate. His desk was clear with the exception of a desk organizer containing a notepad, paperclips, pens, and pencils. There were several files in the letter trays on the credenza behind his desk—each labeled and color-coded.

Adam thought it strange an accountant's office seemed so orderly in the middle of tax season.

"Have a seat, Adam. How are you and Piper holding up?"

"As well as can be expected, I guess. Ann's mom has been a lot of help."

"Well, I've been praying for all of you."

Adam opened his briefcase and removed several folders. "I have both our wills and what I could find on Ann's business."

Bennett took a minute to review the information. "This should do. The first thing we need to do is get Ann's will and the necessary paperwork filed with the probate judge. Probate can sometimes take a fair amount of time to complete, but I see nothing out of the ordinary. I think I have everything here I'll need, so there's no reason for you to worry."

Adam thought, *Nothing out of the ordinary. No reason to worry. Hell, my wife was just murdered!* He controlled his emotions and merely said, "What about Ann's practice?"

"There'll be some state and federal filings but, again, nothing that should present any problems. Her patients will be transferred to Dr. Kate Shaw's practice. Ann and Kate had an agreement that if either of them stopped practicing, the other would take on her patients. Most doctors in private practice have some sort of arrangement like that."

"What else will you need from me?" asked Adam.

"Just your signature on some of the documents and a list of Ann's patients and their files. We should probably get those to Kate in the next week so there's a smooth transition."

Adam saw no reason to get into the fact that Ann's computer and all her patient's session notes were missing.

Bennett continued, "Other than that, there's nothing else you need to do until things settle down."

*Settle down?* Adam thought, *My wife was just murdered, and now he's talking about things settling down!*

"There are some other things I'd suggest you should consider. I think it would be a good idea to have Piper see a professional to help her deal with what's happened. And it may not be a bad idea for you to do the same."

Chief Taylor did mention getting professional help for Adam and his family. It made sense, at least for Piper. "You're probably right, I'll look into that."

"Let me make a suggestion. I think you should talk to Kate Shaw. Piper knows her, and she's familiar with you and the family."

Ann had complained a bit recently about Shaw's tendencies to involve herself in her life. But Piper did know Kate and seemed comfortable around her. "Yeah, she'd probably be better than a stranger. I'll get ahold of her."

"I'd also recommend you make a new will, or at least update the one you have."

Adam nodded his agreement. "Good idea. Anything else?"

"There is, but it's not anything you need to worry about now. Ann's business, while it didn't make a whole lot of money, did provide a consistent income for your family. It paid for Piper's private schooling and helped out with the mortgage payments. Adam, I've done your taxes, and I know your financials. You only have the department's minimum $10,000 death benefit for Ann. That will help, but things are eventually going to get tight for you. Like I said, it's nothing you need to concern yourself about in the short term. But it is something you need to be thinking about."

This caught Adam off guard. Ann had always been the one to pay the bills and worry about money. "Yeah, I guess you're right."

"Let's get some of these other things taken care of first," Bennett said, "Then we can sit down and take a look at your financial situation and some options."

"Thanks, Bill. I appreciate your help on this. You know, I was wondering. You told me Ann wasn't there when you stopped by her office around 3:00, right?"

"That's right. I waited about a half hour. I called her, but her phone went right to message. Kate Shaw's in the same building, and I tried her office, but she never answered her door."

"Did you try calling Ann again when you got back to your office?"

"No. Actually, it was almost 4:00, so I decided to head home."

Adam thought to himself, *Why the hell would an accountant go home in the middle of the afternoon at the height of tax season?*

Bennett stood and they shook hands. "Again, Adam, I'm so sorry about Ann. Let me know if there's anything else I can do to help." They were walking out of his office when he spoke again. "We'll work through this. I'll pray and light a candle for Ann."

Adam froze. *Light a candle?* He managed to thank Bennett again and quickly left the office—his heart pounding like a jackhammer. *Light a fucking candle? Jesus Christ.*

~~~~

Adam wanted to spend as much time as possible with Piper and Tracy before the funeral. Based on Adam's request, McAlister-Smith had arranged a short private graveside service for family and a few close friends. Adam received calls of support from Chief Taylor and Captain Merchant and several other family friends on Tuesday. Marcus and his wife, Makayla, stopped by late that afternoon with dinner and stayed a few hours. After they left, Adam, along with Tracy, Piper, and Max sat on the back porch and watched the sky change from a shade of rust to blood red and finally to a deep blue-black. Night descended on the Holy City as did the realization that their lives would be forever changed.
~~~~

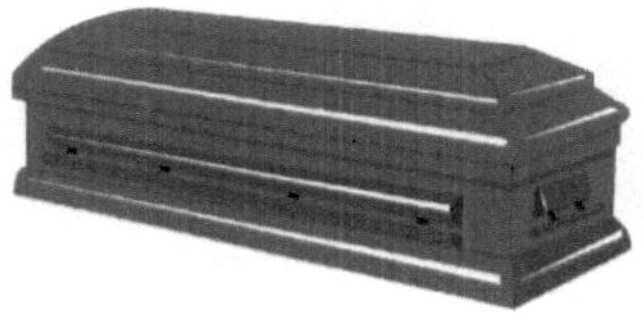

# CHAPTER SIX

Wednesday, March 7

THE MORNING SKY was covered with dark, low-moving clouds when Adam, Tracy, and Piper left for the short drive to Holy Cross Cemetery. They passed through the ornate wrought iron gates and followed the narrow black-topped road as it meandered through the cemetery. Ancient oaks graced the grounds—standing like sentries guarding the graves. The scent of freshly cut grass hung in the morning air. You could hear the quiet. Adam pulled to the side of the road and parked. The ground rose gently to where a velvet-enclosed casket sat next to a freshly dug grave. Their mood was somber as they were lost in thoughts of Ann as the daughter, mother, and wife she was to each of them.

Marcus and Makayla were the first to arrive, followed by Dan Taylor and Ed Merchant. There were gentle hugs and quiet words as others began to assemble. The service was simple but tastefully done. As the last of the morning dew evaporated, the pastor read scripture while adding both humorous and serious anecdotes about Ann.

Adam heard little of it—his mind focused on Ann and the life they'd shared. He couldn't comprehend a life without her. He also couldn't shed the feeling that he was responsible for her death.

As the service was concluding, Adam, Tracy, and Piper each placed a white rose on Ann's casket.

The group lingered after the service, each person offering his or her condolences and adding their own thoughts about Ann and her life. Adam was getting ready to leave when he felt a hand on his shoulder. He turned to see Dr. Kate Shaw looking up at him.

"What a lovely service, Adam."

"Thanks, Kate. I'm glad you were here. I know you and Ann were friends."

"Yes, we were. I want you to know I'm here for you. Please let me know if I can do anything to help you through this."

"I appreciate that. I was actually going to call you. I was wondering if you might meet with Piper and help her deal with all this."

"Of course. Just call me when you get a chance and we'll talk. I'm absolutely free for you both." Kate hugged Adam—she held tight even after he began to let go. She gave Adam a soft kiss on his cheek, and whispered, "Call me."

~~~~

The post-funeral reception at The Citadel was due to start at noon, and Adam arrived early to make sure everything was set up. There was a bar serving wine, beer, and soft drinks and tables with an assortment of light hors d'oeuvres. Adam had given McAlister-Smith a series of photos of Ann at different stages of her life, and they'd created a tasteful collage of the pictures at the hall's entrance. Adam lingered at the collage, each picture bringing back a memory—photos like their first trip together to Hilton Head, their wedding and reception at Boone Hall Plantation, and Ann holding Piper for the first time shortly after she was born.

Adam stayed at the front door welcoming guests and receiving their solace. Well over a hundred-fifty people attended. Despite the questions swirling around Ann's death, the event was more of a celebration of Ann's life than the finality of her death. It was approaching 3:00 when things were beginning to wind down. Chief Taylor pulled Adam aside and put his arm around him. "I want you to think about taking some time off. These past four or five days have been hectic for you and your family. When this thing begins to settle in, you're going to have to be there for them."
~~~~

"Thanks, Dan. I appreciate the thought, but I need to stay busy."

"I heard about Salazar's brother hanging around your house," Taylor said. "I also heard that you refused the suggestion of having an officer stationed there. I'd like you to reconsider, at least until we find out if the Bloods played a part in this thing—especially Vincent Salazar."

"Piper will be back at school next week. Ann's mom will pick her up after school, and I plan to be at home when she gets there. Plus, she'll be staying at our house for at least the next several weeks to help out. If I have to be somewhere else at night, I'd feel more comfortable having Marcus around if that's all right with you."

"I'm okay with that," Taylor said, "as long as you two can cover your cases until we get a better handle on the situation."

"Thanks, chief. I appreciate that."

$$\sim\sim\sim\sim$$

The balance of the week passed with Piper reluctantly returning to school the following Monday. She'd been withdrawn and uncommunicative, spending much of her time alone in her room. Tracy picked her up every day after school and stayed at Adam's house for another few weeks. It was also arranged that Marcus would be at the house if for any reason Adam couldn't be there at night.

Charles Manson worked nonstop on the case over the next several weeks, and it wasn't for lack of effort that little progress was made in identifying Ann's killer. Even with the mounting pressure being put on the Bloods, nothing developed on that front either. The detectives, along with a team of officers, used the files from Ann's office to follow up with each of the patients she had been treating. But without her notes, observations, or diagnoses, it was exceedingly difficult to uncover anything useful. One lead after another found its way to the proverbial dead-end. It was frustrating for everyone involved—these kinds of investigations have a way of sweeping the other areas of your life aside.

Of Ann's thirty-some active patients, most opted to make the transition to Kate Shaw's practice.

Adam tried to put up a positive front for Piper's sake, but his frustration with the lack of progress on the case continued to grow.

# CHAPTER SEVEN
### Saturday, June 2

~~~~

DAYS TURNED INTO weeks, and weeks into months. Still there were no real leads. The investigation had hit a brick wall. Results of the forensic investigations carried out at the murder scene, Ann's Fiat, and her office generated little helpful information. As time passed, departmental demands made it increasingly difficult for Detectives Charles and Manson to spend all their time on the case. A murder investigation is like a shark—it needs to keep continuously moving forward or it will die. As much as the department was committed to finding Ann's killer, her case was slowly becoming "cold." Despite
~~~~

Chief Taylor's warning, Adam, along with some help from Marcus, continued to investigate Ann's murder, but his results also led nowhere.

After about a month staying with Adam and Piper, Tracy moved back to her own house. However, she still spent most of her time at Adam's house. With Ann gone, she had become even more deeply embedded in Adam and Piper's lives. She continued to pick up Piper every day after school and would stay with her on those nights Adam had to work late. As time passed, Piper began spending more time in her room and less with her friends. Adam also withdrew from his previous life—often working late into the night at the station. Ann's death weighed heavily on both of them. Ann was never far from their mind, and they regularly spent time at the cemetery to be close to her memory.

Dr. Shaw met Piper every week for the first few months after Ann's death. Piper gave her permission for Dr. Shaw to update Adam on her progress. At first, Adam met Kate every week or so at her office. But on Kate's suggestion, their meetings were soon moved to a restaurant near her office. Even when the sessions with Piper ended, Shaw went out of her way to remain connected to Adam and his family. At first, Adam thought it was good for her to have the support of an adult female in addition to Tracy. However, his opinion began to change when Piper told him she was starting to feel uncomfortable with Dr. Shaw and wanted to stop seeing her.

~~~~
~~~~

Charleston Collegiate had their annual end-of-the-year award ceremony and silent auction the first Saturday in June. Kate asked Adam if it would be okay if she joined them at the event. Adam thought it would be an appropriate way to thank her for the emotional support she'd given Piper. Her visits to Kate Shaw's office had ended well over a month ago, but Shaw was still calling Piper several times a week and had pressed Adam to continue their weekly lunches. Adam hoped this evening would begin the process of moving away from Kate Shaw's involvement in their life.

Kate lived in a small, two-bedroom, two-bath house in West Ashley, and when Adam picked her up that Saturday evening, he was somewhat surprised at how she was dressed. The conservative garb Kate wore when meeting with her patients was replaced with a low-cut black evening dress that complemented her figure and left little to the imagination. Her hair looked as if it had just been salon-styled, and her perfume gave off an earthy scent of musk.

Tables in the school's gym displayed the variety of items available to bid on in the silent auction—everything from caps and Tee-shirts carrying the Charleston Collegiate logo to all expense paid ski trips to Aspen were available to the highest bidder. Most parents were extremely well off and far from shy about showing it during the auction.

As soon as they arrived, Piper disappeared in search of her best friend, Sophia Parker, leaving Adam and Kate to wander through the treasure trove of items for auction. There was an open bar, and Adam got himself a beer and a scotch and soda for Kate. They were enjoying themselves, debating which vacation package or original piece of art they'd bid on—if only they had money to spend. The award ceremony and dinner wouldn't start for another hour or so, and Kate took advantage of the open bar. Adam was still nursing his first beer when Kate ordered her third scotch. Adam noticed she was getting a little tipsy and suggested they get some fresh air before dinner. Kate gave him a devilish smile and told Adam to stay put, and she'd be right back. She returned in a few minutes, and as they were heading outside, she slid her arm through Adam's, leaned into him, and whispered, "I just made a bid for a dinner for two at High Cotton."

Adam felt uncomfortable with both Kate's physical closeness and intimate tone in her voice when she mentioned the 'dinner for two.' There was no question that she expected Adam to be part of that 'dinner for two.'

Before leaving the gym, she asked Adam to get her another scotch, but he convinced her that the fresh air would do them both some good. The evening was cool but pleasant, and by the time they went back inside for dinner, Kate seemed a bit subdued. Adam found Piper, and they all took seats at a table with Sophia's parents, Mike and Nancy Parker. For a catered event of this size, the meals were excellent, and Adam enjoyed his conversation with the Parkers. He made a point to explain that Dr. Shaw had helped Piper deal with the loss of her mother, and her presence this evening was a way of thanking her for her work with Piper.

Dessert was being served, and the awards ceremony was about to begin when Adam noticed Kate's seat was empty. He assumed she'd gone to the restroom, but when she returned to the table, he noticed she was holding another glass of amber-colored liquid. Her drinking this evening reminded him that she normally had a few drinks at their weekly lunches to discuss Piper's emotional progress.

After a short welcoming from the principal, the trophies and plaques were distributed with Piper receiving two awards—one for academic excellence in science and one for her success on the soccer field. When the awards ceremony finished, the winners of the silent auction items were announced. Adam was surprised and somewhat concerned to learn that Kate's bid of $500 had, in fact, won her the dinner for two at High Cotton.

After the auction winners had been announced and the crowd began to thin out, Adam gathered up Kate and Piper and made the twenty-five-minute drive to West Ashley. Once back at her place, he walked Kate to the entrance to her house. "Thanks for coming, Kate. I'm sure Piper appreciated it."

"I'm sure I appreciated it," Kate giggled. She put her hand on Adam's chest and kissed him on the cheek. Her words were slightly slurred, "I had a swonderful time. We needs to do this again."

Adam hoped Piper hadn't seen Kate's little public display of affection from her vantage. The last thing Piper needed was to see her therapist acting this way. Adam knew his daughter well enough to know that her silence on the ride to West Ashley was a clear indication she was again wrestling with the loss of her mother. Adam was perpetually worried that any little knock could again send her spiraling into a tailspin. Kate Shaw's actions that night only confirmed the need to quickly begin distancing them from her.

Despite his efforts, Kate persisted in her attempts to ingratiate herself into their lives. Back when Ann was alive, she'd sometimes talk about Kate and their relationship. She had always considered her a colleague and little more. Whatever friendship they had was based solely on their being in the same field and working in the same building. They would grab lunch on occasion and traveled together to industry association meetings a time or two. But their interactions began to change over the last year. Kate had taken an increased interest in Ann's family life. She was constantly talking about how lucky Ann was to have such a wonderful and loving husband and an intelligent, creative child. She seemed jealous, and it got to the point where Ann began feeling uncomfortable around her. She began popping up randomly, too, when they were out to dinner or a movie. Adam hadn't paid much attention to this, but the drunken night at the school brought back memories of how strange her behavior had become.

It came to a head a few weeks after the evening at Charleston Collegiate when she showed up at one of Piper's soccer games. Adam told her how much he appreciated what she had done for them but that it was time for all of them to move on with their lives. His work was demanding more of his time, and Piper was busy with her summer soccer league and spending time with her friends.

Kate didn't take it well. "So that's how it's going to be? All of a sudden, you're too busy for me? Well, I don't think so. We have something special, Adam. And you know it."

"Please, Kate. We can still be friends. It's just that Ann flashes back when Piper sees you. I think it would be best if you would leave us out of your life for a while."

Kate was quiet for a moment and then simply smiled and walked away.

It had only been a few months since Ann's murder. Shaw had been seen in public hanging around him and Piper. And the more he thought about the way Kate had come on to him the evening of the silent auction, the more concerned he got. He'd been cleared of playing any part in Ann's death. But the last thing he needed were rumors that he was having an affair with Kate Shaw.

They didn't hear a word from Shaw for several weeks until Adam and Tracy were seated with a group of parents watching another one of Piper's Saturday afternoon soccer games. Adam spotted her standing alone at the far end of the field. She only stayed a few minutes and then was gone, but he noticed he'd received some leery stares from a few mothers. It wasn't the last time that summer that Kate popped up at one of Piper's games or was seen randomly driving past their house. And then there were the late-night phone calls that started early that summer. They'd come at all hours of the night and when he answered, no one was there. He made a point of letting Charles Manson know of her strange and persistent actions.

Adam often puzzled over how someone so screwed up could work in the mental health industry.

~~~~

Just as Bill Bennett had warned, Adam was finding it increasingly difficult to keep up with the bills. Tracy helped as much as she could, but without the income from Ann's practice, it became clear something had to be done. It came down to paying the mortgage or covering the cost of Piper's tuition at Charleston Collegiate. Piper was a truly gifted child and had excelled in the private school environment. Adam didn't want to put her into a new school and be around new students who'd want to know about her mother's murder. The decision was simple—sell their James Island house.

The real estate market had heated up, and the house sold shortly after it was listed. In the meantime, Adam had been looking for a new place to live and decided on Johns Island. Charleston Collegiate was located there, and Piper could still take advantage of the private school's bus service. Knowing Tracy would often be spending the night with them, Adam leased a three-bedroom, two-and-a-half bath apartment in a development just over the Johns Island Connector. It was still only ten minutes from Tracy's and a short fifteen-minute drive to the Lockwood station. The James Island house closed, and they were settled in their new place by late February—almost a year to the day of Ann's murder.
~~~~

~~~~

*The car came to a stop. It was quiet except for the occasional rustlings of the night creatures. The moonlight glistened off the calm water of the lake, as the woman was carried to the edge of the water. She was carefully laid at the base of an oak tree, the drug keeping her mind sedated and unaware of her surroundings. A small portion of her blond hair was removed and placed in a plastic bag for safe keeping. A candle was put in her cupped hands and lit.*

*A soft voice whispered, "The angels are coming to take you to heaven."*
~~~~

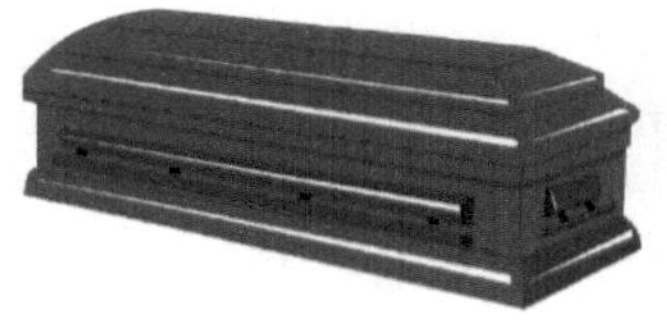

# CHAPTER EIGHT

Friday, March 1

IT WAS FRIDAY, March 1st—the one-year anniversary of Ann's death. Standing in the dark, waiting for his eyes to adjust to the dim morning light, he felt a vague, distant sadness as a gentle breeze wandered through the oak trees that surrounded his apartment complex. The air was cool and colored with a faint scent of the marsh. The moonless sky was speckled with stars. The cicadas and tree frogs were still asleep, and the world was quiet as dawn eased its way into the day, turning the night sky a subtle shade of bluish-gray.

It had been a difficult year—a year without Ann. Piper was now thirteen and would be finishing eighth grade in a few months. Adam couldn't believe how she'd grown, both aca-demically and socially. He was proud but always worried. Adolescence brought with it its trials and tribulations, and it was clear to Adam she continued to suppress her grief. But it still would come out at times. Ann's death still affected her just as deeply as it had Adam and Tracy, and they relied on each other in dealing with their life without Ann.

Adam was watching night surrender to dawn when Piper joined him on the patio. He saw her eyes were moist. She'd been crying. "Come here, sweetheart," he said, wrapping her in his arms.

"I miss her."

"I know, baby. I know. We all do."

"I can't believe it's been a year, Dad. We should do something special tonight."

"Good idea. We could take Tracy out to dinner at the Fat Hen tonight. She loves the place."

"That would be nice, and she can come to my games tomorrow."

"Go ahead and get ready for school. I'll make some break-fast. Your bus will be here at 6:45."

After getting her fed and off to the bus, he dressed and headed downtown, stopping at the Coffee Cup on his way in. The coffee at the police station tasted like it came straight from Jiffy Lube, and he had gotten in the habit of picking up coffee and croissants for himself and Marcus.

"There you go," he said, putting a coffee and roll onto Marcus' desk.

"You're a good man, Charlie Brown," Marcus said with a smile. Marcus was aware of the significance of the day. "Listen, why don't you and Piper join Makayla and me for dinner tonight?"

"Thank you, my friend. That's nice. But I'm taking Piper and Tracy out to dinner."

As the day went on, most everyone in the department acknowledged the significance of the day and offered their heartfelt support to Adam.

~~~~

Dinner that evening was enjoyable and for the most part upbeat as they all shared special memories of Ann. Adam told of how he'd been so nervous the night he asked Ann to marry him that he dropped the ring—a story they'd both heard numerous times. They reminisced about their annual vacations to Hilton Head and laughed about the disastrous, rain-soaked camping weekend at Myrtle Beach. Tracy's eyes misted as she spoke of how similar Piper was to Ann at her age. All in all, it was a good night—one filled with positive memories of their life together.

The morning came up pink and gray as Adam left for his weekly roundball games. His hands were slick with sweat, but he maintained his vice-like grip on the ball. It felt good to have something to hold onto. These Saturday games had been for years his therapy for dealing with the stress and demands of his job, and now they helped him grapple with the continuing
~~~~

trauma of losing Ann. After his games, Adam picked up Tracy and headed over to Piper's round-robin soccer tournament.

Piper's team won all three games, and Adam was especially thankful they made it through without Shaw making one of her unannounced appearances. For the most part, she'd stopped showing up at Piper's games, but the late-night phone calls and hang-ups continued. Even though she lived in the Ashely River area, Adam sometimes ran into her at the grocery store or gas station. He was always civil but kept the encounters as short as possible. He had hoped Kate had gotten the message, but he wasn't within five miles of being sure of it. Her erratic behavior and apparent problems with drinking led Adam to wonder just what she might be capable of. It was clear Kate Shaw hadn't given up on her infatuation.

Piper was spending the night at Sophia's house and left with the Parkers after the games. He dropped Tracy off and as he said good night, he realized he was finally ready to confront something he'd been putting off for a while. He and Charles Manson had gone through their house after Ann's murder looking for clues but found nothing. It had been a year since he'd packed up Ann's things, and he felt like maybe he was finally ready to deal with them.

After his nightly walk, Max joined Adam as he opened a bottle of wine and queued up the Eagles' Greatest Hits. Most of the boxes were labeled "Clothes" with a few others containing Ann's jewelry and an assortment of other personal items. He would keep some of her clothes and other things that brought back special memories, but he was ready to donate most to Goodwill. He opened the first box and was immediately overwhelmed by the scent of his wife—light and sweet, orange and bergamot from the Versace perfume he'd always given her on her birthday, Valentine's Day, and Christmas. He held one of her dresses to his face and breathed in the memories—bringing back a wave of emotion from the ebb and flow of their life together. Ann's scent was not lost on Max either. He buried his nose in her clothes and wagged his tail. He hadn't forgotten her, either. At times, Adam's eyes moistened and everything around the edges of his field of vision took on a soft glow. He took his time, separating items that would hold special meaning for Tracy, Piper, and him.

The wine had taken a firm hold by the time he opened the last box, filled with Ann's jackets and overcoats. He was almost finished sorting through them when he felt something in the pocket of one of the coats. He reached in and found two flash drives. "Old" was written on one drive, "Current" on the other. He could barely believe it. All this time, right there in the box.

Adam felt a jolt of energy. There was no doubt in his mind that these were the backup drives for Ann's patient folders. They would contain a record of all her session notes, descriptions, and diagnoses for both her old patients and those she was treating at the time of her death. They may hold clues to why Ann was murdered and who might have done it. He knew he needed to get these drives to Charles Manson, but he also realized that they might not be totally forthcoming about what was on them. Right now, the case was dead in the water, and there was no way he was turning the drives over before he knew what was on them.

This room would be his home office, and his computer was already set up on his desk. He inserted the drive labeled "Old" into one of the USB ports. A list of what must have been well over a hundred folders appeared listed in alphabetical order by the patients' last names. He moved the files onto his desktop, then inserted the "Current" drive. Just as he had expected, approximately thirty more folders appeared identifying the patients under her care when she was killed.

The files were color-coded. Each patient name was highlighted either blue, yellow, or red. Adam knew Ann had coded her patients based on the severity of their condition. A "Code Blue" patient had been diagnosed and was being treated for a relatively mild psychological condition. A "Code Yellow" patient carried a more moderate diagnosis, and their treatment normally required a more structured and a longer length of treatment. A "Code Red" label identified a patient suffering from more serious mental health conditions. These would require both the use of prescription drugs and intensive psychological counseling.

The great majority of her current patients were "Blue." Three were "Yellow" and two "Red." The first thing that came into Adam's mind when he thought of the designation Code Red was the movie, *A Few Good Men,* and the memorable Code Red dialog between Tom Cruise and Jack Nicholson. But that was a movie—this was definitely not. These Code Red patients were real-world people with very serious mental health problems—problems that would automatically target them as suspects in Ann's murder!

Adam was about to investigate the Reds but froze when he saw the name, Katherine Shaw, classified as a Code Blue.

*Jesus Christ, Ann was treating Kate Shaw!*

Then he remembered that it wasn't at all unusual for a psychologist or psychiatrist to have their own therapist. He opened Shaw's file and began to read. Based on her notes, Ann had been treating her approximately six months for alcohol dependency and something called Possessive Personality Disorder (PPD). It all made sense—her drinking at their lunches and at the awards dinner. And she certainly displayed examples of possessive behavior directed toward Adam and Piper. This could explain many of Kate's strange actions over the last year.

He closed Shaw's file and moved on to the two Reds. Both were men—Charles Knight and Tyler Scott. Adam opened Knight's folder first. He was a thirty-three-year-old groundskeeper for Charleston's county parks system. He was diagnosed with moderate paranoid schizophrenia. Ann was working with another physician and using a combination of weekly therapy sessions and antipsychotic medications. His folder contained his initial diagnosis, evaluation, and treatment plan.

Patient Name: Knight, Charles
Initial Evaluation: 06/14/2017
Initial Diagnosis: Paranoid Schizophrenia—moderate
Treatment: Cognitive Behavior Therapy and medication

<u>History:</u> Charles Knight is a single thirty-three-year-old male.

<u>Initial Symptoms:</u> Visual and auditory hallucinations, persecutory delusions, confused thoughts, difficulty concentrating, and disorganized speech. Some weight loss. Difficulty sleeping. Insomnia reported. Impulsive behavior.

<u>Severity/Complexity:</u> Moderate.

<u>Suicidality/Self-Injurious:</u> Denies suicidal ideas or intentions. Denial is convincing. No history of self-injury.

<u>Past Psychiatric History:</u> First symptoms reported to have begun in the patient's early 20s.

<u>Withdrawal History:</u> No history of withdrawal from any psychosomatic medication.

<u>Psychiatric Hospitalization:</u> None

<u>Outpatient Treatment:</u> Received outpatient mental health treatment for anxiety. No medication initially prescribed.

<u>Psychotropic Medication History:</u> Antipsychotic medication started approximately six months after initial outpatient treatment—Lurasidone 25 mg (3X daily) Increased to 50 mg (3X daily) Current dosage maintained with Chlorpromazine (200 mg 3X's daily) and Zofran. Seems to be good compliance with medical instructions including medication orders.

<u>Addiction/Use History:</u> Denies history of substance abuse.

<u>Social/Developmental History:</u> Lives alone. Difficulty interacting with people. Trust issues. Symptoms result in difficulty holding consistent employment.

<u>Family History:</u> Father deceased. Known to have had anxiety issues. Sister lives in Seattle. Thought to have depression. Treated as outpatient for a learning disorder. Family psychiatric history otherwise negative. No other history of psychiatric disorders, psychiatric treatment or hospitalization, suicidal behaviors or substance abuse in closely related family members.

<u>Medical History:</u> Adverse Drug Reactions: List of Adverse Drug Reactions: (1) Added ADR to Penicillin, Reaction(s) = Respiratory Distress, Status = Active.

<u>Allergies:</u> No known allergies.

<u>Diagnosis:</u> Adjustment disorder with moderate paranoid schizophrenia, F43.21 (ICD-10) (Active) Generalized anxiety disorder, F41.1 (ICD-10) (Active) Histrionic personality disorder, F60.4 (ICD-10) (Active)—displays mild to moderate OCD symptoms.

<u>Instructions / Recommendations / Plan:</u> Weekly outpatient treatment setting is recommended because patient is impaired to the degree that there is interference with interpersonal /occupational functioning.

<u>Psychopharmacology Supportive Therapy:</u> Maintain current levels of Chlorpromazine (200 mg 3X's daily) and Zofran. Begin 6.25 mg Ambien for insomnia (monitor monthly).

<u>Electronically Signed By:</u> Ann Stone: 1/14/2018, 5:23 p.m.

After he finished reviewing Knight's file, Adam moved onto Tyler Scott's. He was a baggage handler at the airport and displayed signs of borderline personality disorder (BPD). He Googled the disease and learned it is characterized by impulsive behaviors, intense mood swings, feelings of low self-worth, and problems in interpersonal relationships. The treatment called for intensive cognitive therapy supplemented with a substantial dosage of antipsychotic drugs. Scott was receiving, 400 mg of Seroquel and 200 mg of lithium twice daily. There was one major difference between the diagnoses of Knight and Scott. The BPD diagnosis is associated with an increased risk of violence and impulsive behavior. Physical aggression is one of the diagnostic criteria for BPD. Scott's BPD, like severe cases of schizophrenia, could lead to violent outbursts and a high level of anti-social behavior. Several serial killers, including Ted Bundy and Jeffrey Dahmer, were diagnosed with severe cases of BPD. A note in Scott's file indicated he also suffered from something called Inhibited Sexual Desire (ISD)—a medical/psychosomatic condition completely different from erectile dysfunction (ED). Adam remembered one night when Ann had teased him that people with serious mental illness would sometimes lose the desire for sex.

He was surprised that there were no addresses or phone numbers in the patient files. That information would have been kept in Ann's filing cabinets, and Charles Manson had those folders. There had been a concerted effort to locate and interview Ann's patients. However, with no specific information on the type and severity of their illnesses, it was difficult to establish any definite links to the murder. But now Adam had that information, and he wondered, *Where are Knight and Scott now? Are they being treated by Kate Shaw? Are they being treated at all? Had they ever been arrested?* He dug into the files for the next few hours but could uncover very little that answered those questions.

He opened the "Old" drive and learned that there were four Code Red patients whom Ann had treated in the past. He reviewed each patient's diagnosis and treatment notations, but found no information indicating when or why they had left treatment or their current mental status. It was clear he needed help.

Lockwood had some good tech officers. But while they were good, they were somewhat limited in the methods they could use to extract data. They had to work under the constraints of warrants and within an acceptable legal framework. But Adam had another resource—one free of such legal constraints.

Like he had done with Jayden King, Adam had caught and turned a computer hacker by the name of Chester Wood. Wood lived in the dark and murky underbelly of the web where the world of hackers could be divided into the Black Hats and the White Hats. Black Hats are the really bad ones. They'll steal your identity, spread viruses and malware, and involve themselves in a whole range of other nasty and destructive mischief. Although it sounds like an oxymoron, the White Hat hackers are the good guys. Chester always said he was sort of a Gray Hat—somewhere in the middle. He had his own code of ethics and displayed a conscience only when it was convenient to have one.

Adam always wondered why people like Chester chose to become hackers. They were definitely smart, and their computer skills would be valuable to big business or the government. Maybe they felt socially inept. Maybe they dropped out because of the hypocrisy they believed permeated big business and government. Whatever the case, he was glad he had access to his talents.

Chester Wood had some legit clients, but they were few and far between. Most of his work was done for what might be called the criminal element. Like many cities, Charleston's government was not totally run out of City Hall. Big business CEO's and certain criminal bosses asserted their own brand of dominion over the city. A few years ago, Chester was hired by some underworld types to plant child pornography in the work computer of a local politician. Chester knew most all the politicians but could not give a shit about politics. Someone once said that talking politics to Chester was like talking to a fire hydrant. Chester planted the child porn, tipped off the cops, and the career of the politician came to an abrupt and embarrassing end. Adam kept Chester out of the bust, and by doing so, he added a world-class computer hacker to his stable of snitches.

Adam rummaged through his desk and found two flash drives. He copied Ann's drives onto his computer and then downloaded each of them to the extra flash drives. A day earlier, the investigation had been dead in the water. Now he may have found the break he'd been looking for. Adam needed to catch a few hours of sleep before he would see his snitch, Chester Wood.

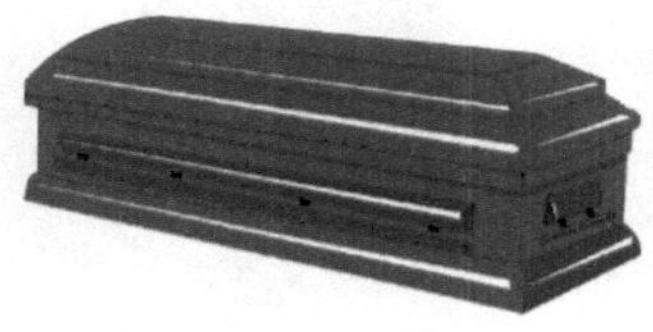

# CHAPTER NINE

Sunday, March 3

SOPHIA'S PARENTS WERE taking Piper to Sunday brunch and wouldn't drop her off until about 1:00 p.m. This would give Adam time to stop by Chester's one-bedroom basement apartment on Spruill Avenue close to the old Navy Shipyards in North Charleston. North Charleston had several upscale neighborhoods, but this was definitely not one of them. After taking Max on his morning walk, he took the Crosstown to I-26, exiting onto Spruill.

It was still early, but Adam knew the time of day meant little to Chester, who almost never left his place. He'd usually nod off in front of his array of computer screens, sleep for a few hours, and then dive back into his digital malaise. He could have been the poster boy for the prototypical computer hacker. Adam pounded on the door several times until he finally heard a series of locks being opened. A mousey-looking girl opened the door. Her face showed the remnants of her battles with adolescent acne—the acne obviously winning the war.

"Good morning, Nora. Is Chester around?"

"Yep." She locked the doors after letting him in. The small apartment was dark and smelled like fast food. Chester Wood was seated behind a sea of electronics.

Wood wore a gray hooded sweatshirt covering a mop of long black hair. He weighed around 125 pounds and looked like Tom Waits on a bad day. He was a squirrely little shit. He may have lacked an acceptable level of hygiene and ignored basic social norms, but he was a wizard with his computers and a damn encyclopedia when it came to criminal groups and their players in and around Charleston.

"Good morning, Chester," Adam said as he wound his way through the spaghetti maze of cables and wires connected to an impressive display of high-tech and obviously expensive computer equipment.

Without even looking up, Chester answered, "Detective."

Adam asked him what he was working on, but before he could answer, Nora piped up, "He's workin' on some Russian stuff."

"Ukrainian," Chester corrected, "Not Russian."

"Yeah, he's workin' on some stuff from Ukrainia."

"No," Chester said.

"No, what?"

"It's not Ukrainia. It's Ukraine."

"Yeah, smartass," Nora retorted, "so why'd you call the stuff Ukrainian if it's not from Ukrainia?" She plopped down in one of the two bean bag chairs—the only other furniture in the room.

Eyes still glued to the computer screens, Chester said, "What'd you want, Stone? I've got some important stuff I need to finish. Make it quick."

"Relax," Adam said, "don't be such a drama queen."

"I'm not a drama queen, Stone."

"Yeah, Stone," Nora said, "I can vouch for him. Chester's not gay most of the time."

"That's good to know, Nora." Adam turned back to Chester. "Look at me, Chester." He stopped pecking on his keyboard and looked up at Stone. "I've got some people I need you to check out."

"Shit, Stone. I'm in the middle of something. Why don't you use your own techies?" Chester grinned, "Oh, wait. I know. They suck."

"No, Chester, they don't suck," Adam calmly replied, "and I seem to remember you're the one who got caught. Now, I want you to shut up and listen. This has to do with my wife's murder."

Before Adam could continue, Chester said, "Sorry, Stone. Go ahead. What'd you need?" Despite being one of Stone's snitches, Chester actually liked him. Adam explained that the two flash drives he found contained information on Ann's patients, and there was a chance that one of them could have been involved in her murder. He went on to explain the way Ann color coded the patients based on the severity of their mental condition. "It's been a year since the killing, and the department has come up with virtually nothing. I want you to background the Code Red patients. Oh, and yes, I'm giving copies of the flash drives to our own techies down at Lockwood, so you've got some competition."

Chester laughed and said, "You call that competition?" Wood, like most world-class hackers, could be annoyingly arrogant when it came to their abilities. Adam put up with his idiosyncrasies knowing that Chester could accomplish in an hour what would take Adam days. Chester smiled and said, "Consider it done."

~~~~

Adam returned home where he finished organizing Ann's things. He separated the items he would give to Piper and Tracy and those he would keep for himself. He boxed up the remainder and drove them to the local Goodwill store.

He hadn't been back long before the Parkers dropped off Piper. After taking Max to the dog park, Adam and Piper returned home and ate a light dinner. Piper had a paper due Monday and spent the rest of the evening typing it up. Adam poured himself a glass of what was left of the wine he'd opened the night before. He sat on the patio wondering if his discovery
~~~~

of the flash drives might lead to solving the mystery of Ann's murder.

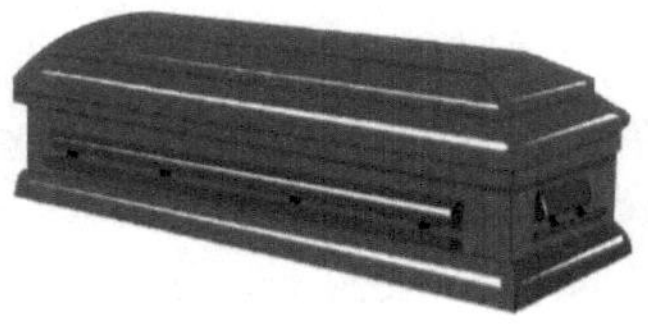

# CHAPTER TEN

Monday, March 4

FIRST THING MONDAY, Adam hurried into Taylor's office to tell him about the drives. Taylor's face was grim throughout, and Adam was about to accuse him of not giving a shit when the chief cut in.

"Adam, there's been a development that you need to know about."

Taylor went on to tell him there had been a murder outside of Atlanta with eerie parallels to Ann's.

"About a week ago, something new popped up on the NCIC. A young nurse by the name of Camila Hanson was murdered outside of Atlanta around the Jackson Lake area.

Local officers were making their rounds through the park and found her body in a remote area of the lake. There were similarities between her murder and Ann's—throat was cut, and a candle left near her body. They sent us the autopsy results, and there wasn't any propofol in her system. However, she was drugged with sodium thiopental."

"Shit, Dan. You should have told me."

Taylor let the comment slide without response.

"After talking to Atlanta, we agreed to keep the details of what happened under wraps. We don't want the media to get a hold of the specifics. This is our first break in the case, and the last thing we need is the press making noise about a possible serial killer. That'll tear this city apart at the seams."

Taylor paused to let his comment sink in. "I'll get those flash drives to Charles Manson and our forensic psychologists. They'll follow up on whatever's in them. These may be the breaks we need, but we have to be careful not to let them get out to the public. Let Claire and Matt run with it, and I'll tell them to keep you informed this time around. But remember, all this needs to stay quiet."

"Chief, I want you to make it clear to Charles Manson that I get access to anything they have out of Atlanta and whatever the psychologists find on those drives." Adam said this knowing he had his hacker snitch, Chester Wood, chasing down the patients on Ann's flash drives.

"I'll do that," replied Taylor. "They can use you, but I still don't want you in the field. You'll know what develops, but they need to run their own investigation."

Adam stood and placed the flash drives on Taylor's desk. "Thanks, Chief. I'll do that. I just need to be part of this thing. And one way or another, that's exactly what's going to happen."

~~~~

Adam went straight to the Kennels. Claire and Matt were having coffee and were somewhat surprised to see him. Their interactions had lessened because of the lack of progress in the investigation.

"Good morning, Adam," Matt said.

Adam made no reaction, and there was an awkward silence until he finally said, "Listen, I know you two are working the Atlanta murder. Where are you on that?" Neither Claire nor Matt said anything. "Damn it, the chief just sent me up here. He gave the go-ahead for me to work with you. Just tell me what you've got so far."

Manson nodded to Charles and Claire said, "We've only been on the case less than a week. When we learned there was a candle found at the crime scene, we contacted the Jackson Lake and Atlanta detectives to coordinate the investigation. When we learned the extent of the similarities to Ann's murder, Chief put a lid on any details getting out to the press."

It was clear Adam was still pissed that the whole thing had been kept from him. "Well, I know it now, so fucking enlighten me."
~~~~

"All right take it easy," Matt said, "Here's what we've got so far. The victim's name is Camila Hanson, and she was a nurse at Emory Hospital in downtown Atlanta. Apparently, she'd been dead for a few days before she was found in Jackson Lake Park. The animals had gotten to her, so the crime scene was compromised. Her throat was cut, and a candle was found next to the body. We think there's a decent chance she was killed by the same person that murdered Ann. Now you know why we needed to keep the details quiet. You can imagine what the media would do with this."

Adam had several more questions about the Atlanta killing before he told Charles Manson about the flash drives. "Taylor will get those to you. He wants you to work with one of our forensic psychologists to see if there's anything on them that would link one of the patients to Ann's murder. He wants me in on whatever they come up with."

"We'll do that," Claire said, "but there's something I just don't get—the timing of the two murders. They're almost a year apart. That seems like a long time for the killer to wait."

"Maybe so," Adam said, "but it's not unusual for serial killers to wait a length of time after their first victim. The problem is that the time between their kills tends to get shorter and shorter. Speaking of killers, anything new on the Bloods? I know we haven't come up with much on them, but they're still a suspect as far as I'm concerned."

"Agreed," Mason said, "They were initially at the top of our list of suspects. Eye for an eye thing for you offing Cedric Salazar. But it's been a year since that happened, and we've come up with nothing on them. Plus, we don't see any apparent connection between them and the nurse killed outside of Atlanta. I'd say they're no longer one of our primes."

"I agree with Matt," Claire said. "Unless something else comes up, I'd say we're looking at either one of Ann's patients or a serial killer."

It had been over a year since Ann's death, but Adam still felt the ache in his heart listening to the detectives analyze her murder. He continued to feel responsible for her death and the pain it caused everyone involved. He had remained uneasy with both Kate Shaw and Bill Bennett, but Charles Manson felt they had already cleared both of them, and Adam kept his suspicions to himself.

"We'll stay on this, Stone," Manson said. "Hopefully, we'll get the results from the flash drives within the next day or so. We'll let you know as soon as we do."

Adam stood, an indication the conversation was over, and he returned downstairs.

~~~~

Back at his desk, Adam told Marcus about his discovery of the flash drives and the murder of Camila Hanson.

"This will definitely get everyone off their ass and kickstart the case," Marcus said, "And talking about getting off asses, I just got a tip on our own case from my contact in the Posse. If you want to stay on Ann's case, I can follow up with that myself."
~~~~

"No, we'll do this thing together." Adam quickly responded, "Let's go."

Marcus shook his head. He knew arguing with Adam would be a losing proposition. Finally, he said, "All right. Come on, partner." Stone slid his Glock 19 into its spine holster and clipped it onto the back of his belt. He grabbed his windbreaker and followed Marcus.

Adam and Marcus had been investigating a narcotics distribution case involving a gang called the East Side Posse. Marcus was point on the investigation. A series of drug overdose deaths had occurred over the last month or so in the eastside of the Charleston peninsula. The deaths were traced back to a batch of fentanyl-laced heroin. The case was similar to Devon Jackson and the Bloods' investigation the year before.

It seemed many of the users had no idea the heroin was laced with this potent opioid, and the result often led to these fatal or near-fatal reactions. The East Side Posse controlled the drug trade, prostitution, and loansharking in that part of downtown. Like Adam, Marcus had his own group of snitches, and one was a Posse member named Mikey Brown. Mikey was your typical gangbanger—big gun and little brain. He told Marcus the Posse was getting the laced drugs from the Sinaloa Cartel—via the Port Authority's North Charleston Terminal. Marcus and Adam were working to identify the person who was coordinating the shipments from Colombia and spent the rest of the day and most of the next chasing down Mikey Brown's lead.

~~~~

It was income tax time, and Adam had arranged a Wednesday afternoon meeting with Bennett. He arrived with an armful of paperwork, and as soon as he entered Bennett's office, he did a double take when he noticed a dark gray smudge on Bill's forehead. He caught himself staring at it. "Sorry, Bill. I forgot it's Ash Wednesday."

Bennett crossed himself and said, "Ah, yes. The dust from which God made us all. The beginning of Lent, so we can fast and cleanse the world of evil."

Adam had never been completely comfortable around Bennett. Adam was not a religious person, but he never had a problem with anyone showing their faith. But Bennett seemed a bit over the top. Charles Manson had vetted Bennett shortly after the murder and found nothing incriminating, but Adam was never able to shake his comment of "I'll pray and light a candle for Ann" much less his recent "cleanse the world of evil" comment. He made a mental note to have Chester do some more research into Bennett's background.
~~~~

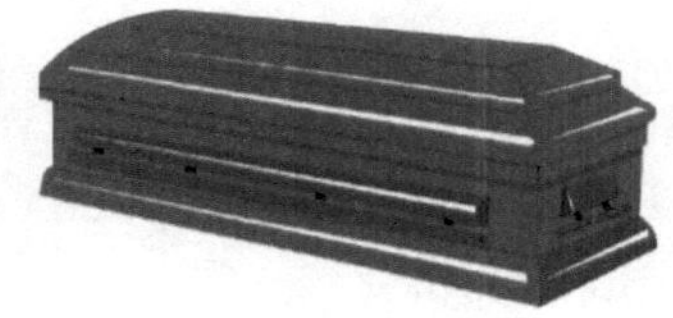

# CHAPTER ELEVEN
Thursday, March 7


THE DRUG INVESTIGATION had kept Stone busy, but now the possibility of a break in Ann's case dominated his mind. It had been a year of frustration with little if any progress made in finding Ann's killer. One of Ann's patients had always been a suspect, but without the flash drives, there hadn't been much to pursue. However, the discovery of the drives and the murder of Camila Hanson breathed new life into the investigation.

It was midafternoon Thursday, and Adam and Marcus were having lunch in the downtown Wendy's on Meeting Street. Marcus had just finished his burger and asked Adam if he'd heard back from the psychologist about the patients listed on the flash drives.

"Nothing."

"I still can't convince myself the Bloods weren't connected in some way to Ann's killing," Marcus said, "Even though it's been a year since you took out Cedric, I still say there's no way his little brother would just let that sit."

"I'm not saying they're not in the mix," Adam agreed, "and I also suppose it could've been some random sicko." But Adam believed chances were slim Ann's murder was a random act. Money, sex, and jealousy were the usual motives for murder, and the killer was almost always someone known to the victim. He was leaning toward one of the Code Red patients, but he couldn't shake thoughts about the unusual behavior from Kate Shaw and Bill Bennett. He was due to see Chester Wood that night and would have him look into both their backgrounds. It had also been some time since he'd talked to his Bloods' snitch, Jayden King. He needed to follow up on that, too.

~~~~

Adam and Marcus called it quits around 5:00. Adam had arranged for Tracy to stay with Piper that evening until he got back from his meeting with Chester.

Nora let him in. "Chester, any luck with the flash drives?"

"Luck has nothing to do with it, detective."
~~~~

"Whatever," Adam said. "Did you get anything on those patients?"

Before Chester could answer, Nora laughed. "Did he get anything? Hell, Stone, does a bear piss in the woods?"

"Shit," Stone said.

"Shit?"

Adam shook his head. "Shit, Nora. It's 'Does a bear *shit* in the woods?'"

"Yeah, well they probably piss, too."

Adam looked at Chester. "Help me here, Chester."

"Shut up, Nora," Wood said. "The answer is yes. And the two current Code Red dudes are certifiable nutcases. Hang on a second." He swung around to another keyboard and screen and brought up his notes.

"Okay, let's look at Knight first. He's the one with schizo-phrenia. He was taking 50 mg of Lurasidone three times a day. That's a pretty typical dosage for someone with moderate para-noid schizophrenia. He's the one being treated by Dr. Shaw."

"How do you know that?"

"I got into her computer through her website. No big deal. She has a cheap piece of shit McAfee antivirus software. By the way, the other guy, Tyler Scott, isn't being treated by Shaw anymore. Anyway, Knight was born and raised in Atlanta. His mom took off shortly after he was born, and he was raised by his dad, who worked for the railroad as a night watchman. The old man committed suicide when Knight was eleven, and he spent the next seven years in the system. Sister lives in Seattle. He enlisted in the Army right after high school but left after his four-year commitment. His file said the family had its share of mental illness, and he was first treated for anxiety and depression in his mid-twenties. He's had several run-ins with the law, but all have been fairly minor. No arrests for the past several years. After he got out of the Army, he had a string of menial jobs in Atlanta until he moved to Charleston. He worked at the Parks and Recreation Department for two years but left about six months ago. I couldn't find out where he works now. As far as I can tell, he still lives in an apartment at 2002 Bolton Street in North Charleston."

"It doesn't seem like there's been any violence in his background," Adam said.

"You're right, but that's sure as hell's not the case with your Tyler Scott."

"What do you mean?"

"First of all, his file showed he was getting 400 mg of Seroquel and 200 mg of lithium twice a day. That's enough to put a water buffalo asleep. You probably don't want to think about what might happen if he goes off his meds. He was born in Youngstown, Ohio in 1980 and lived there until his mid-twenties. He tried to enlist in the Army, but never made it past the mental health screening and was rejected. I couldn't find much about him until he was arrested and convicted for armed robbery in 2010 in Cleveland. He spent four years in prison for that. He had a few minor arrests until he moved to Charleston in late 2016. He worked at the airport until he was let go about a year ago. I couldn't find where he's got any current employment. He's living in an apartment in the Brentwood section of

North Charleston." Chester grabbed a folder from the table behind him and passed it to Adam. "All the information I found on both guys is in here. Now can I get back to work?"

"What about those old Code Red patients?"

"Still working on that. Now, can I please get back to work?"

"Sure, Chester, right after you get me everything I need." Adam handed Chester the names, addresses, and a short write-up on Dr. Kate Shaw and Bill Bennett. "I need info on these people, too."

"Christ, Stone!"

"I'll pick all the stuff up tomorrow after work." Adam left without another word.

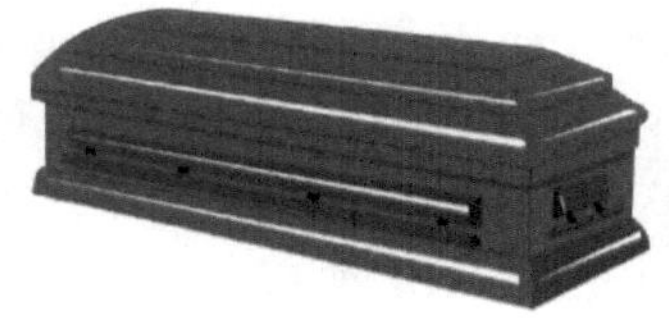

# CHAPTER TWELVE

Friday, March 8

PIPER WAS SPENDING the night at Sophia's house Friday, so Stone had the apartment to himself. Chester had come through with his research that afternoon on the old Code Reds and background on Shaw and Bennett. After making a pot of coffee, Adam retired to his office to review what Chester had given him.

There were only four of Ann's old patients that carried a Code Red designation. Chester amassed a good amount of information on these individuals, however, none seemed to have posed a threat to Ann. One had passed away, one was serving a five-year prison sentence for armed robbery, and two had moved away—one to Idaho and one to California.

Also, there was nothing in the backgrounds of either Shaw or Bennett that raised any serious red flags. Shaw grew up in Summerville, received her undergraduate and doctoral degrees from the University of South Carolina and had worked for the VA for three years prior to starting her private practice in 2005. The only thing somewhat unusual was the fact that she'd been married twice. Her first marriage ended in divorce after less than a year. Her second husband died tragically when he fell while vacationing with Kate in the Grand Canyon. She'd lived in her West Ashley house for the past ten years, held memberships in all the typical psychiatric associations, and rarely missed her weekly Pilates class.

Bennett was born and raised in Atlanta. His father was a pastor at Wheat Street Baptist Church. After a four-year stint in the Army with two tours in Afghanistan, he returned to the States where he received a business degree from Emory University. Three years later, he earned his CPA license while working at Ernst and Whinny. It seemed that his time in the service only deepened his devotion to his faith. He led prayer groups during his time overseas and assisted the company chaplain. When he finished his commitment to the Army, he moved to Charleston and became an elder in the Mt. Pleasant's First Baptist Church and remained active in its ministry. After his parents' death, he used his inheritance to open his accounting business. Bennett never married and lived alone in a small house in Mt. Pleasant.

None of this information was going to bring Adam closer to finding Ann's killer. He felt stuck again, but hopefully the break was coming with the Atlanta investigation.

Adam had lost track of time digesting the information Chester had given him and had to smile when he saw Max sitting by the front door. He'd been patiently waiting for his evening walk. His tail went into overdrive when Adam grabbed his leash and said, "Come on, boy."

It was overcast but otherwise pleasant when they left the apartment. The moon was just a rumor, peeking out every so often from behind the night clouds. It was quiet except for the occasional rustling in the woods from the night creatures making their rounds. The pungent smell of the marsh hung heavy in the air. He was lost in thought, his mind bouncing between what he'd just received from Chester and the drug investigation he and Marcus were running.

He'd been walking Max for about five minutes when the bullet slammed into his left shoulder. It spun him around, and he hit the sidewalk hard. He was dazed and confused when he looked up and saw the barrel of a snub-nose .38 pointed at his head.

Behind the revolver was the sadistic face of Vincent Salazar. "I've been waiting a year to take you out, motherfucker."

But before he could pull the trigger, Salazar suddenly disappeared from view, and the gun flew up in the air—landing a few feet from where Adam lay. He turned is head to see Max on top of Salazar, his teeth embedded in his right forearm.

Adam grabbed the gun, got to his feet, and kicked the side of Salazar's head like he was going for a game-winning 50-yard field goal. Adam knew the first rule of street fighting is that there are no rules.

Salazar was out like a light, and Adam wrestled Max off him. He was on his knees holding Max's collar when he saw another man running away. Whoever it was tripped on the curb and fell face-first in the street, but he just as quickly scrambled up and disappeared into the night. Stone's head ached from where it had hit the sidewalk, and his arm was bleeding profusely, but he managed to pull out his cell and call 911.

"This is Detective Adam Stone. I have a code 10-00—officer down. Address is 224 Fenwick Apartments off Maybank on Johns Island. Suspect disarmed and under control. I've been hit. Please hurry!"

"Okay, detective. Stay where you are and remain on the line. I'm dispatching officers now."

It was only a matter of minutes before two Johns Island squad cars arrived on the scene. The officers were out of their car, guns raised, "Stay down! Don't move!"

Salazar was still out cold. Adam's jacket was soaked red with blood, Max at his side barking loudly at the four officers. "Down, Max. Down, boy." He finally got him settled down enough for the officers to cuff Salazar. Adam pointed toward where the second man had disappeared. "There's another guy. He took off that way." One of the officers made it all the way to the entrance to the apartment complex, but by that time the second man was long gone.

Once the code for "officer down" was broadcast, it didn't take long for six more patrol cars to show up, sirens wailing and blue and red lights illuminating the night. Apartment lights were flicking on, and tenants were coming out to see what the commotion was about. A short time later, an EMS van pulled up, and two paramedics jumped out and began attending to Stone's arm and the nasty cut above his right eye where he'd hit the concrete.

Adam was giving a statement to the police when he started to feel dizzy. A wave of nausea hit him, and he passed out.

~~~~

Adam opened his eyes. The room was quiet and the light dim. He glanced at his right arm. It was heavily bandaged but didn't hurt. Everything in the room glowed softly. He felt mellow. Then he saw Marcus and Chief Taylor standing at the foot of the bed.

"Well, look who rejoined the living," Marcus said.

Adam felt a hand on his left shoulder. "Detective Stone, I'm Doctor Hull. You're going to be fine. The bullet nicked your brachial artery, and you lost a good amount of blood. You also have a mild concussion, but no internal bleeding. We got you all patched up now, and you should be good as new in a few weeks. I'm keeping you at the hospital tonight, but you'll be discharged tomorrow morning. You'll need to come back in a week or so to get the sutures removed. Get some rest now, and I'll see you in the morning."
~~~~

Adam thanked the doctor and asked if anyone had contacted his daughter and mother-in-law.

"They were here earlier," Marcus said. "But you were sleeping. They just left but will be back here first thing in the morning to take you home."

"What happened with Salazar?"

"Don't worry about him," Taylor said. "He's going to be hit with attempted murder, plus a list of other charges too long to mention. With his rap sheet, he'll probably get somewhere between 10 and 20 years."

"He said it was payback for taking out his big brother," Adam said, his face showing the bitter aftertaste of retribution.

"Listen," Taylor said, "you heard the doctor. You need to get some rest."

"Thanks, guys." His eyes still feeling heavy. "I am feeling kinda loopy. I think I'll get some sleep now."

Marcus patted Adam's leg. "Sleep tight, brother. We'll catch you tomorrow."

~~~~

Tracy and Piper arrived at the hospital early the next morning. Piper gave him a hug—careful not to jostle his arm which was heavily bandaged and in a sling.

"Does it hurt a lot, Dad?"

"Feels better now that I see my little girl."

After Dr. Hull signed his discharge papers, Tracy drove Adam back to Johns Island. Piper had to hold back Max when
~~~~

he saw Adam. They all made their way inside and Adam said, "Sorry, sweetheart, I don't think I'll make your game today."

"I don't have to go, Dad. I can stay here if you want me to."

Adam smiled and gave his daughter a kiss on the forehead. "I'll be fine. Tracy will take good care of me."

"Mrs. Parker told me she could pick me up. Are you sure it's okay, Dad?"

"I'm sure. I'm sorry I can't be there. Win one for the Gipper."

"Who's the Gipper?"

"Never mind. Have fun and play well."

Piper left, and Adam convinced Tracy he'd be fine. She left a short time later, and he spent a quiet afternoon watching NCAA March Madness until his cell rang. He figured it would be Tracy or Marcus checking up on him. "Hello."

"Oh, my God, Adam! Are you all right? I heard you got shot. I'm on my way over."

"Jesus Christ, Kate. No, I don't want you to come over. I'm fine. Wait a minute, how'd you know I got shot?"

"Piper told me."

"What do you mean Piper told you?"

"I'm at her soccer game. Really, I can bring dinner. Do you need anything?"

Adam was trying to keep his anger under control when he clenched his teeth and said, "Listen to me, Kate. I told you that you need to give us some space. You need to move on with your life and so do we."

"Don't be upset. I'm only trying to help."

He was quiet for a moment. He couldn't believe that it had been months since he'd heard from Kate, and despite the late-night calls, he thought he was basically free of her. He'd never been rude to her but had made it clear that he wanted her to stay away from his family, especially Piper. But her call had chased away the last vestiges of hope that she intended to leave them alone. He was pissed.

"Stay away from my daughter and don't call me anymore!" He ended the call and spiked the phone into the couch. A sharp pain shot up his arm.

*Damn, just what I need!* He thought about calling Sophia's mom to check on Piper, but figured their game was probably over, and she'd be driving her home by now.

His arm ached. He hoped he hadn't torn any stitches and took two pain pills which began working in short order. He slowly began to feel more under control. Mrs. Parker dropped off Piper about forty-five minutes later. He'd calmed down by then and decided not to mention anything about Shaw. Soon afterward, Tracy showed up with dinner, and they all ate listening to Piper talk about the game.

The balance of the weekend passed quietly without anything further from Kate Shaw.

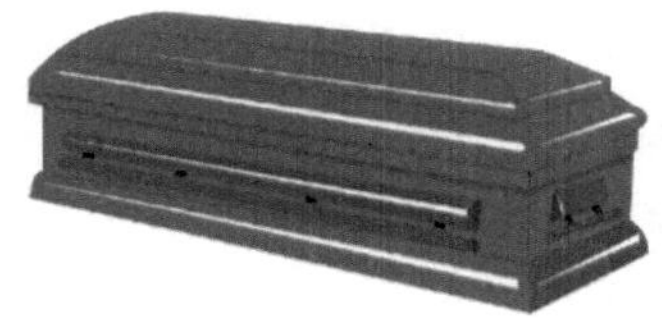

# CHAPTER THIRTEEN

Monday, March 11

THE DOCTOR HAD ordered Adam to stay home for a few days, but he would have none of it. After Piper left for school Monday morning, he dressed and drove downtown. His arm was in a sling, the pills keeping the pain to a minimum.

"Christ, Stone," Taylor said. "What are you doing here?"

"I'm fine. Did the psychologists come up with anything off the flash drives?"

"I don't know. Charles Manson's in. Check with them."

Adam went upstairs to the Kennels where he found Claire Charles and Matt Manson. "Good morning, detectives."

Claire saw the sling, "What the hell, Stone? We heard about what happened at your place Saturday, but we sure didn't expect to see you today."

Adam told them about Salazar's attack and how Max saved his life. Claire smiled and said, "Well, I hope to hell someone gave that dog a few extra bones!"

Adam planned on seeing Jayden King later that day about what happened but definitely didn't want the detectives to know. "I don't know whether the Bloods sanctioned the hit or if Salazar was acting on his own accord. Either way, he's looking at some serious prison time."

"I'd be surprised if he did it without an okay from their shot caller," Manson said. "If he did, he better watch his back in or out of prison. He may have just been a soldier, but he probably knew enough to cause the Bloods some problems if he decided to play 'Let's Make a Deal' with the prosecutor."

"You're right," Adam said. "Vincent may be an asshole, but he's not stupid. My bet is he keeps his mouth shut."

He spent another twenty minutes with Charles Manson discussing the investigation before heading downstairs.

Marcus saw him and shook his head. "I figured you were too stupid to stay home and rest."

"I missed you, too, partner," Adam said, with a hint of a smile. "What do we have planned today?"

"I thought I'd lean on Mikey some more. I think he knows more than he's given us."

"All right, but before we do that, I've got a favor to ask."

"Shoot."

He told Marcus about the second man he saw when he was attacked. "I've got someone inside the Bloods. His information has usually been spot-on, and I wanted to see if he knows anything about who was with Salazar when he shot me."

Marcus grinned. "We all have our secrets. I don't need to know who your guy is, but I've got my own mole inside the Bloods." He held up his hand, picked up his desk phone, and dialed a number. He waited a moment and then said, "Gee, sorry. I must have punched in the wrong numbers." He hung up.

"All right, I give up. What was that all about?"

Marcus continued to grin and told Adam to wait. A minute later his cell rang. He picked it up, listened for a few seconds, and said, "Question for you. Who shot the cop Friday night? Yeah, I know that. Who was the other guy?" Another moment and then, "Thanks. Be safe."

"That was your snitch?"

Marcus nodded. "He said the guy with Salazar was another Blood named Jayden King."

Adam's face fell. He felt like he'd just been punched in the stomach. "Oh, shit." He gathered himself and told Marcus that King was his covert contact inside the Bloods. He kicked himself for not considering the possibility that his death would be Jayden's ticket out.

"Looks like he was working both sides. You've been played, brother."

A darkness fell over Adam. "That son of a bitch!"

"Hey, buddy. Shit happens. What do you want to do about it?"

A strange smile appeared on Adam's face. "I'm going to pay a visit to my friend, Jayden. Here's what I want you to do."

~~~~

It wasn't until the third time Adam drove by the BP station that he saw Jayden. He seemed apprehensive, but a slight nod of Jayden's head confirmed he'd seen the tap on the outside of the Charger's door. Thirty minutes later, Jayden pulled into the Citadel Mall, stopped next to the Charger, and rolled down his driver's side window. Adam saw the cut on his forehead and the bruised knuckles on the steering wheel. He got out and leaned against the side of his car, just staring at Jayden.

Finally, Jayden said, "Shit, Stone, I don't know what's up with Vincent, man. Nobody does. I heard the cops got him." He saw the sling. "Are you all right?"

"I'm fine. Thanks for your fucking concern. Now get out of the car." Jayden stepped out of the Chevy and faced Adam who continued, "I just have one question, and I need a straight answer. You lie to me, and I'll take your ass down. Did Vincent act on his own, or was he sent by your people?"

Jayden quickly answered, "He did it on his own. I told you we had nothing to do with any of this. You're not a target anymore."

"I need the name of the other guy that was with Vincent when he shot me."
~~~~

"I don't know what you're talking about. Word is Salazar did this by himself. All I know is that as far as the Bloods are concerned, it's done. It's over, Stone. Vincent went rogue, and that's it."

Stone's dark eyes were hollow and unforgiving. "Over? No, Jayden, this will never be over for me." He pointed to the corner of the lot. "See the black guy in the white Crown Victoria over there?" King saw the car. Adam waved at the Crown Vic and said, "Smile, Jayden, you're on Candid Camera." Adam slid back behind the wheel, put the Charger in gear, and slowly drove away—leaving Jayden King alone in the parking lot.

~~~~

Back at the station, Marcus downloaded the shots he'd just taken. They clearly showed King and Stone together in the mall's parking lot. He printed three 8" X 10" color prints.

Later that afternoon, Adam drove to the corner of Ashley Phosphate and Stull Road, parked next to the BP, and rolled down his window. It didn't take long for one of the prostitutes who worked the corner to saunter over. She bent down, displaying her ample cleavage. "Hi, handsome. You lookin' to party?"

Adam opened his wallet and removed two one hundred-dollar bills. He gave her the money and one of the color prints. "Here you go. Money's for you. Give the picture to Jayden. Tell
~~~~

him it's from his good friend, Detective Stone, and one of these is on its way to his shot caller."

She was confused but not about to question the two Benjamins in her hand. "All right, sugar. Whatever floats your boat." He waited as she went inside the station. A minute later, Jayden came out and saw Adam in his Charger. Adam couldn't hear him but could clearly read his lips. One word: "Shit."

Adam never saw Jayden King again. He disappeared. Some say the Bloods took him out. Some say he took off and was in the wind. Stone would put his money on option number one.

On the way back to Lockwood, he took a call from Bill Bennett. He'd finished Adam's tax returns and needed him to stop by his office to review and sign. Adam agreed to stop by the following afternoon.

When Adam arrived at Bennett's office the next day, he signed the returns and was about to leave when Bennett stopped him.

"There's something else, Adam."

"What's that?"

"Well, I met with Dr. Shaw the other day. She was dropping off her tax info and mentioned something, and I got the feeling she wanted me to tell you. Maybe it has something to do with Ann's case."

"What'd she say?"

"It's kind of strange. She said there's been a man hanging around her office for the past week or so. He shows up around 5:00 p.m. and just stands across the street, never stays for more than five or ten minutes. He's always wearing an army jacket and one of those camouflaged baseball hats."

"Well, she needs to call the police."

"That's exactly what I told her, but she said she didn't want to get the police involved. She said the man was probably just waiting for a bus."

"I doubt the guy is waiting for a bus. The only stops around there are at the corner of Wesley Drive and about a half mile down Savannah at West Oak Forest Drive. Neither stop is anywhere near her building."

"I thought maybe you could talk to her," Bennett said. "You know, convince her to do something. Call the police."

*What the hell,* Adam thought, *she's probably using this to try and get back in my life again.* The last thing Stone wanted to do was call Kate Shaw. But the situation did sound strange, and apparently it hadn't been a one-time thing. The guy was hanging around there for a week—maybe more.

"All right, I'll talk to someone at the station and have them check it out. But don't tell Dr. Shaw you talked to me about this."

"Okay. Maybe it's just her imagination. She can be a bit strange at times, but I felt like I had to share."

"You were right to tell me, Bill. Like I said, I'll have someone from the department look into it."

*Maybe the guy was stalking Kate. Maybe it was one of Ann's old patients. Could this have something to do with Ann's murder? Why didn't she want to get the police involved? Maybe she just made the whole thing up.* Adam left Bennett's office late that afternoon and was taking the Crosstown when he decided to swing by Kate Shaw's building. He pulled into a parking lot a few houses down from her building in a position to watch the area across from it. Late afternoon traffic had picked up, and about twenty minutes later, he saw him—army jacket and camouflaged cap. The man leaned on one of the streetlight poles and stared at Shaw's building, periodically glancing at his watch. Adam waited a few minutes before exiting the Charger. He started crossing the street when one of the cars slammed on its brakes and blew his horn. The noise got the man's attention. He must have seen Adam because he started running away. After a few near misses, Adam made it across the road and took off after him. His arm, still in the sling, slowed him down. The man disappeared into a medical building, and when Adam got there, he was nowhere to be found.

~~~~

Adam stopped by the hospital Wednesday morning to have his stitches removed. The arm was healing nicely, and he'd already regained virtually all its range of motion. He arrived at Lockwood and went straight upstairs to the Kennels where he found Claire Charles at her desk. He told her about the guy he'd seen hanging around Shaw's office.

"I chased him, but he got away. I checked with the desk sergeant and found out Officers Johnson and Dailey cover that area. They're on the eleven-to-seven dayshift. I'm going to have
~~~~

them check it out. This might have something to do with Ann's case."

"Maybe," Claire said, "but Matt and I will talk to Johnson and Dailey. Better you don't get in the middle of this stuff. We'll let you know what we come up with."

"You do that." Stone left without another word. He was obviously once again pissed at not being able to be more of a direct part of the investigation into his wife's murder.

When he got to his desk, he told Marcus about the man hanging around Shaw's office.

"This could be something," Marcus said. "I know how desperately you want this to be solved. We all do. Just don't let it push you into doing anything stupid, okay? Do what you've got to do. Just be smart about it. Chief finds out you're in the field sticking your nose in the investigation without Charles Manson he'll probably send you on a vacation. And I don't want to deal with the Posse and the cartel by myself."

Adam, still frustrated, said, "I hear you, partner. Now, what's our plan for today?"

# CHAPTER FOURTEEN
### Friday, March 22

THE FOLLOWING WEEK passed quickly with Adam and Marcus making good progress on the Posse drug investigation. Mikey Brown came through with a name—Miguel Alvarez. Brown said he'd seen Alvarez meet with Odell Davis, the shot caller for the East Side Posse. It was a good guess that Alvarez was Odell's contact in the Sinaloa Cartel.

It was late Friday afternoon, and Adam and Marcus were in a meeting with their contacts at the FBI, Coast Guard, and DEA. They were in the middle the DEA's intel presentation on the fentanyl investigation when Adam's cell vibrated. He slipped the phone out of his pocket and saw the call was from

Claire Charles. He returned it to his pocket. The group took a break about twenty minutes later, and Adam went out of the room to return the call.

"Listen, we just got a call from Dailey about Shaw's building."

"What'd he say?"

"They were making a pass by the building and saw the guy with the baseball cap and army jacket. He was right across the street from Shaw's office. Dailey said when they slowed down, the guy took off running right across Savannah Highway. Two cars almost hit the son of a bitch. When he was running, his jacket flew open, and Johnson said he saw something metal tucked in his belt. He couldn't be sure but thought it looked like a knife or gun."

"Tell me they got him."

"Afraid not. It was rush hour, and by the time they got their squad car pulled over, the guy had made it to the tangle of streets in the St. Andrews area. They lost him in there."

"Shit. That's two times. All right," Adam said. "I've gotta get back in a meeting, but I should be at the station in an hour or so."

The meeting lasted another forty-five minutes. DEA's Captain Robert Francis finished by telling the group Miguel Alvarez was staying at the Hampton Inn on Meeting Street in the downtown's Historic District. "He's been there for about ten days, but no one's been able to confirm Mikey Brown's tip that he has actually met with the Posse's Odell Davis." Captain Francis looked at Stone and Williams. "You two know the local landscape, so it makes sense for you to shadow Alvarez. Learn his routines and let us know if he hooks up with Davis."

Marcus raised his hand. "We've already started, captain. We know he walks everywhere. He never uses Uber or takes a cab. And he also only uses cash for everything including his hotel room. There's a Starbucks a block from the Hampton that Miguel goes to every morning. He buys a latte and a blue-berry muffin and pays with a twenty. We arranged with the manager to have his cash set aside. We all know around ninety percent of our paper currency has traces of cocaine or heroin. We got one of the bills Alvarez used at the Starbuck's and gave it to our lab rats to test for fentanyl. And sure enough, they found a trace."

"That's interesting," Francis said, "but it's not going to connect him with the Posse."

"I know, but there's more. He takes a walk downtown every day and basically follows the same route. He goes up Meeting Street and then over to East Bay and spends some time around the terminal where the cruise ships dock. Then he goes to the Robert Lange art gallery on Queen Street, and here's where it gets interesting. He spends about fifteen minutes looking at the paintings and always ends up upstairs in front of a huge painting by a guy named Nathan Durfee."

The Coast Guard Lieutenant smiled and said, "So I guess Miguel likes big boats and big paintings."

There was a smattering of laughter in the room and Marcus continued, "Maybe so. But I showed the gallery's do-cent photos of Miguel Alvarez and Odell Davis, and she said she's seen them meet a few times at the gallery, always upstairs."

The room got deathly quiet. Then Captain Francis said, "So, are you thinking what I'm thinking?" With a hint of a smile, Marcus nodded. The captain continued, "Get the gallery to let us stash a listening device somewhere around the Durfee painting. With luck, we might catch one of these meetings between Alvarez and Davis."

"That shouldn't be a problem," Marcus said. "We'll take care of it."

Captain Francis looked at his watch and stood. "Good. Let's plan on meeting early next week."

The meeting broke up, and Adam and Marcus walked out into the unusually humid afternoon. "Well, that was fun," Marcus said. "Did you see Francis' face when I told him about the art gallery? That was special!"

"Sure was, Sherlock," Adam said. "Listen, Dailey and Johnson saw the army jacket guy that's been hanging around Shaw's office. They lost him, but they think he had a knife or a gun."

"Jesus," Marcus said. "Can they ID the guy?"

"I don't know. They didn't get a good look at his face, but we have mug shots for Ann's Code Red patients, and if army jacket is one of the patients, they may recognize him."

It was pushing 5:30 by the time they arrived at Lockwood. Marcus wanted to follow up with the mug shots but had promised Makayla he wouldn't work late. Adam dropped him off at his car and met with Charles Manson about securing mugshots of Knight and Scott.

Things had been heating up with both Ann's murder and the fentanyl drug case. He realized he'd been spending a lot of time on the job and felt bad he hadn't been there for Piper. Adam knew Tracy would be at his apartment with Piper and called her. "Hey, sweetheart, how about dinner at the Tattooed Moose? My treat."

"Really, Dad! That would be cool. Granny and I are just sitting around watching TV."

The meal at "The Moose" was the start of a relaxing weekend for everyone. Adam needed a break from the stress of his job. He played hoops Saturday morning with his buddies and then joined Tracy at Piper's soccer game. Sunday was spent watching Michigan State upend Duke for a berth in the Final Four.

~~~~

*The Mustang's headlights were off when it stopped behind one of the huge concrete columns that supported the bridge. The car's engine clicked as it cooled. A steady breeze from the northeast carried the smell of the ocean. The woman in the front seat hadn't moved for some time. She had, however, slid lower in the seat, her dress bunching and exposing a portion of her upper thighs. The hem of her dress was gently pulled down, so it covered her legs. A candle was placed on the dashboard and lit, its light playing off her face. The knife was used to remove a lock of her hair.*

*And then the voice. "It's time to go to heaven."*
~~~~

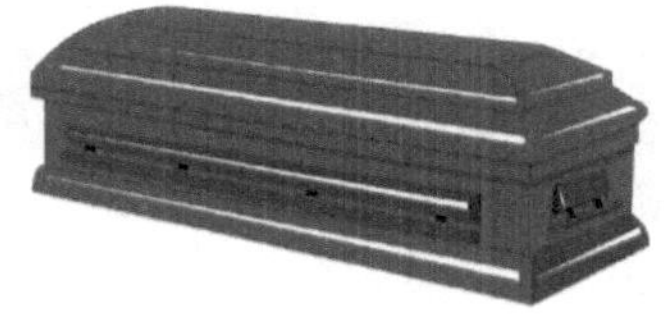

# CHAPTER FIFTEEN

Monday, March 25

ADAM SHOWED UP for work Monday with a sense that big breaks were coming on both the drug investigation and Ann's murder. It felt good, a sensation he realized he hadn't felt since Ann's death. But as he carried the lattes and croissants into the bullpen, he was met with an unusual silence. He asked a detective where Marcus was, and he pointed upstairs. In the Kennels, Adam found Marcus in an intense discussion with a few pit bulls, one of whom saw him coming and nodded in his direction. Marcus turned, and Adam noticed he wasn't smiling—nobody was.

Adam grinned. "Did I miss something? Feels like a funeral around here." His attempt at humor hit a brick wall.

Marcus broke away from the group and put his hand on Adam's shoulder. "I take it you haven't heard."

"Heard what?"

"There's been another murder."

Marcus explained that earlier that morning a 911 call came in from a groundskeeper at Memorial Waterfront Park just over the Ravenel Bridge in Mt. Pleasant. When the groundskeeper arrived, he saw a gray Mustang parked at an odd angle in the grass-covered parking area next to one of the bridge abutments. It was still dark, and he approached the car using his flashlight. When he pointed the light inside the Mustang, he saw a body sprawled in the passenger's seat—a woman, throat slashed from ear to ear. The car's interior was awash with blood that glistened under the glow of the flashlight. The groundskeeper was obviously shocked but managed to get his cell out and make the call.

Stone remained calm and asked, "Was there a candle?"

"Yes. Charles Manson's out there now with several uniforms and CSI technicians. The chief gave the okay for you to go out there as long as you stay out of the way."

"Let's go," Stone said, and headed for the stairs.

"Wait!" Marcus called after him. "I need to meet one of our computer techs at the art gallery. We need to get the microphones embedded before it opens at 11:00. I'll meet you at the park as soon as we're done."

Stone pulled into Waterfront Park, leaving his Charger parked next to several Mt. Pleasant and Charleston police cars. The green and yellow CSI truck was next to the coroner's van. The area had been cordoned off with crime scene tape, and a group of civilians in jogging gear were already rubbernecking behind it. After giving his name and badge number to the crime scene attending officer, Adam saw Matt Manson. Matt waved him over. The white-gloved technicians were still gathering evidence and taking photos in and around the Mustang when a police flat-bed tow truck arrived and backed into position to load the Mustang. It would be transported to the forensic garage behind the Lockwood station where the technicians would complete the forensic examination. Adam was now close enough to the Mustang to smell the coppery scent of blood and see its arterial spray on the dashboard and windows.

"Tell me what we've got here, Matt," Adam said.

"Car's registered to a Sally Richardson. White female, twenty-eight. Lives not far from here on Coleman Boulevard. Throat's been cut. Nasty shit. The coroner's initial estimate makes the time of death between roughly 1:00 and 4:00 this morning. We've got an officer chasing down tapes from the security cameras." Manson pointed over to one of the police cars. "Claire's over there with the worker who made the 911 call. The poor guy's really shook up."

Adam stared at the Mustang and remained quiet for a moment. "Marcus told me there was a candle in the car."

"Yeah. I'm sorry, Adam. It looks like this one has all the characteristics of your wife's murder." Manson glanced to his right and muttered, "Oh, Shit." A Channel 5 News van was pulling into the park. "Just what we need. So much for keeping this under wraps. This town's gonna go apeshit when this hits the street." He told one of the officers to get over there. "Keep that she-vulture behind the tape and away from my crime scene!"

"I'm going over to talk to the 911 guy," Adam said. "You better call Chief Taylor and tell him Channel 5 just showed up. He's gonna want to get out in front of this."

"Got it," Manson said and pulled out his cell.

Adam spent ten minutes with the groundskeeper, but it was clear he had little more than what he'd already told Detective Charles. The flat-bed was driving off with the Mustang, and Adam was heading back over to Manson when he heard someone call out, "Hey, Stone. Hold up!"

He turned and saw Chelsey Wallace, the crime reporter for CBS Live 5. Stone had dealt with her after Ann's death. She was a tough and seasoned reporter with a decent reputation. Microphone in hand, she was jogging toward Stone, cameraman right behind her and struggling to keep up.

"Detective, what's the victim's name?"

"This is a crime scene. Get back behind the tape!"

She told her cameraman to cut the shoot. "Stone, off the record. Is it true this might be related to your wife's murder?"

Adam glared at her. "This is off the record, right?"

"Yes! Give me a break here."

"Well, in that case, no comment!" He shouted to one of the uniforms to get her behind the tape and headed back to

Manson, who'd just hung up his phone. "What did the chief say?"

"He's going to schedule a press conference later this afternoon," Matt answered. "Merchant will handle it. He wants me and Claire there, too. There's a meeting at 2:00 to go over talking points. He wants you there for that one. Not much more we can do here. Claire's already pulled the mugs of Knight and Scott. Maybe one is the guy outside Dr. Shaw's building, and Johnson and Dailey can tag him. We surveilled Knight's and Scott's apartments last year, but I'm going to put an officer on each of them. The department's going to be stretched to its limits when the media breaks the story, but I can't see the chief saying no. I'll let you know about those mugshots."

As Adam was leaving the park, lyrics from *Mustang Sally* floated through his mind. The song had been one of his favorites—not so much now.

~~~~

The meeting to prepare for the press conference started at 2:00 sharp. Chief Taylor, Ed Merchant, Claire Charles, Matt Manson, and Jake Hess from forensics were already seated when Adam and Marcus arrived at the conference room.

"Matt, give us what you and Claire have on the victim," Taylor said.

"Name is Sally Richardson. White, twenty-eight-year-old neonatal nurse at East Cooper in Mt. Pleasant. She's single and lives alone in the Boulevard Apartments on Coleman. That's
~~~~

pretty much all we've got on her so far. The officers are still working on it. Her parents live in Greenville and have been notified. Time of death is estimated at sometime between 1:00 and 4:00 this morning." Manson then recapped the sequence of that morning's events starting with the 911 call from the park's groundskeeper.

"Thank you, Matt," Taylor said. "Jake, what's forensics have?"

"Not a whole lot yet. The footage from the security cameras showed a hooded man carrying a small backpack leaving the area at approximately 2:00. He appeared to be of average height and weight, but it was dark, and the hood covered his face. We're still working the vehicle. It's a 2015 Mustang registered to the Richardson woman. Only prints so far are from the victim. Any trace evidence will be sent for DNA analysis, but that will take time. No weapon has been recovered from the scene. There was heavy blood spray on the dashboard and windshield from a deep, oblique, long incised injury on the front of the neck." Hess pointed to his neck and showed the path the knife would have taken. "The laceration started below the left ear at the upper third of the neck and deepened gradually severing the carotid artery. It's not conclusive, but I'd say the killer was probably right-handed. There were no visible defensive wounds. Hopefully, the autopsy will give us more to work with."

"Okay," Taylor said. "We all know the main components of this murder closely resemble what happened with Ann's case. And some of the characteristics match the murder of the nurse in Atlanta three months ago."

Claire Charles suggested the possibility of this being a copycat killing.

"That's always a possibility," Merchant offered. "But certain specifics of the previous killings were not made public. This one so closely mirrors Mrs. Stone's that I suggest they were done by the same person."

"I think we can agree on that," Taylor said. "I don't have to tell any of you what's going to happen when the media learns more about this. There's been initial broadcasts on TV and radio stations, and social media coverage is already hinting about this being a serial killing. And there's no doubt this is going to hit the national media. I've met with the mayor, and you can imagine his concerns about what this is going to do to our city, especially tourism. We're coming into the peak season, and the longer this goes, the worse it's going to get. I want all inquiries about this to go through Ed's office." He looked at Merchant. "Go ahead, Ed."

"We'll give the press the basics this afternoon but need to limit the specifics as much as possible. Detectives Charles and Manson have been working Ann Stone's case, and they'll be the prime on this one as well. My office is already working on setting up a special "hotline" to handle calls. We want to assure the public that we're doing everything possible, but we can't comment on the details of an ongoing investigation. It's going to get bad out there."

"I've already received calls from the FBI," Taylor said. "They'll be sending in a team including a BAU profiler out of Quantico. They can be a pain in the ass, but we need all the help we can get with this one, so deal with it."

Adam had worked with a lot of FBI agents over his twenty years on the force. Most were topnotch professionals, but there were plenty of egos the size of Yankee Stadium.

The meeting broke up, and Merchant stopped Stone in the hallway. "I want you and Williams to step up work on your fentanyl case. Two more overdose deaths were reported last night. The department's taking heat for it, and with the Richardson killing, it's only going to get worse."

"I know," Adam said. "We're set up with those seed microphones in the art gallery. The staff will let us know if Alvarez or Odell Davis show up. Plus, We also have an officer reviewing the daily recordings. I feel like a break is coming."

"Good. Listen, Adam, I know this is going to be a tough time for you and the family. We'll get the bastard, but you need to—"

Stone interrupted. "I know. It's Charles Manson's case. I get it. I've been hearing that for the past year. Christ, Ed, I've been a cop for twenty years, and you're telling me to stay on the sidelines. I can't do that anymore."

Merchant was quiet for a time. Finally, he shook his head and said, "All right, Adam. Consider yourself in, but you're still to work with Charles Manson. No cowboying on this. Understood?"

"Understood," Adam replied.

~~~~

Tracy had left that morning to visit a friend in Greenville, and with everything that had happened that morning, Adam had forgotten to call her. He got ahold of her, told her what had happened, and that she needed to come back home. It was about a four-hour drive which meant she wouldn't get back until after 6:00 that evening. He'd already planned on picking up Piper after school.

Adam knew the Richardson murder would be compared to Ann's killing, and he needed to prepare Piper and Tracy for the onslaught of media attention that was definitely coming their way. Things had taken a drastic turn—he was finally ready to have an officer stationed outside his apartment.

Adam watched the press conference in the bullpen with a handful of detectives and uniformed officers. It went as well as could be expected ... despite the painful series of questions linking this murder to Ann's. The phrase "serial killer" was even used a few times when questioned by the media. The press conference ended, and he drove off to get Piper at Charleston Collegiate.

He pulled up to the roundabout at the school, and Piper got in. He sensed a heaviness on her. "Dad, I heard about that lady that got killed this morning. Everyone's saying it's just like Mom."

"We're not sure about that, honey. But we just want to be a little more careful until we understand what's happening."
~~~~

"Can I still go to my soccer game this week?"
"Absolutely. And Granny and I will be there, too."

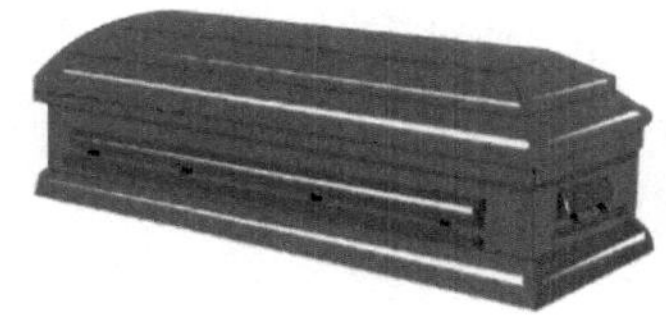

# CHAPTER SIXTEEN

Tuesday, March 26

AS EXPECTED, THE media coverage of the Sally Richardson and Camila Hanson murders had indeed gained momentum and was now dominating the airwaves and social media. Nancy Parker and several others had called the night before pumping Adam for more information on the killings and what the police intended to do about them. And Piper seemed more apprehensive of the situation having also gotten calls from her friends at school. The last year had been dominated by Ann's death and its investigation, and it had obviously taken its toll on the family. Now the wounds were opening up again.

Adam parked his car and was about to enter the station when he was hit with a wave of emotion. *Why did this happen to us?* He'd asked himself that question thousands of times and thousands of times it was left unanswered. The sun was not up yet, but there was enough ambient light to make out the surroundings. His eyes were drawn to the park across the street. He wasn't ready to deal with what he knew was waiting for him in the station and made his way to the park. There was a gazebo near the banks of the Ashley River where Ann would sometimes join him for lunch on her day off. He sat there with his eyes closed, lost in those memories.

"You all right, partner?"

He turned. "I'm okay. Just needed a break."

"I hear you."

Marcus sat next to Adam. Nothing more was said. Nothing needed to be.

A few minutes later, Adam stood. "Let's get at it." They walked to the station in silence.

As they entered, the desk sergeant told Adam there was a meeting getting started in the conference room, and Merchant wanted him there.

Merchant and Charles Manson were seated at the conference table along with another woman Stone didn't recognize. She was dressed in a conservative dark blue pantsuit, had short brown hair, and looked to be in her mid-forties.

"Come on in, Stone," Merchant said and nodded toward the woman. "Adam, this is Mary Wells. Mary, meet Detective Adam Stone. He'll be sitting in with us this morning. Ms. Wells is a criminal profiler and will be working with us on the Richardson murder. She arrived last night from Quantico."

Adam shook her hand and took a seat.

"Nice to meet you, detective. As I was just telling everyone, I've had a preliminary briefing on the Richardson killing and wanted to give my initial impressions on the case. I'm aware that the previous two murders have characteristics in common with Ms. Richardson's case and that your wife was one of the victims. Also, I have had an initial discussion with the Atlanta detectives working the Camila Hanson case."

Before she could continue, Merchant asked her to detail her background and provide some general information on serial killers. "Despite Charleston's reputation as a historical and cultural center, we certainly get our share of murders. Obviously, most are drug-related. We've all been around police work for years, but most of us have never dealt with cases where a serial killer might be involved."

"Certainly," Wells said. "First some basic background. I have both undergraduate and graduate degrees in sociology and psychology from Brown University. I spent about six years as a parole officer in New York City before I was accepted in the FBI school at Quantico. I've spent the last thirteen years in the Behavior Analysis Unit there. My title is Supervisory Special Agent. In plain English, I'm what's known as a criminal profiler.

"I am aware that one of your local gangs, the Bloods, and some patients that had been treated by Mrs. Stone are suspects. However, I'm here because many of the elements of these murders indicate a high probability that they may be the work of a serial killer. It may not be, but it's my job to view it as such and help you find the person who did it.

"Before I get into my thoughts on these specific cases, I want to give you some general identifiers that indicate the possible existence of a serial killer. While there have been well known female serial killers, about 95% are men. These serial killers rarely change the way they kill unless they're forced to. At the FBI, we've defined four distinct types of these killers based on the way they plan and carry out their murders. Understanding each category makes it easier to investigate their crimes and bring them to justice." Wells stood and wrote the names of the four categories on a whiteboard. "We define the four groups as Power and Control, Visionary, Missionary, and Hedonistic.

"The Power and Control serial killer derives sexual gratification from domination and humiliation. Most famous serial killers we have seen in history and the media would fall into this category.

"Visionary serial killers feel compelled by voices or visions they experience. Many of them believe they have been instructed by God or the Devil to kill.

"A Missionary serial killer is the third category, and they feel a need or duty to kill certain types or classes of people. Prostitutes are often a target of this type of killer.

"The last classification, Hedonistic killers, have a strong connection between personal violence and sexual gratification. These are lust or thrill kills. They receive pleasure from the act and eroticize the experience. They differ from the other three groups in that they spend little if any time planning their kills."

"Which group do you think our killer might belong to?" Merchant asked.

Mary Wells smiled. "Well, I have my thoughts on that, but I'd like to hear from all of you first. Based on what you know about the murders, what group do you think our killer falls into?"

Ed looked around the room and said, "I guess I'll start. Well, I don't think he's Hedonistic. There's no evidence of rape or sexual exploitation, and the murders seem to be well planned."

"I agree," Wells said. "How about you, Detective Charles?"

"I'd probably eliminate Power and Control. Again, I don't see a sexual element to any of the three killings. Plus, all the victims work in the medical field, so it could be the Missionary one you mentioned. Adam's wife was a psychologist, and the last two were nurses."

Wells looked at Matt. "Detective Manson, your thoughts?"

"I agree with Claire. They're all violent but not in a sexual way. Plus, there's the candle, so it could be a religious thing. I'd probably go with the Visionary type."

Wells nodded her agreement. "Detective Stone?"

Adam was quiet for a moment. Finally, he said, "I'm only here to observe. I'd rather not say."

"That's understandable," Wells said. "From what I've learned so far, I'd have to agree with all of you. The violence seems controlled, and I don't see sex or lust involved. The medical connection suggests this could be Missionary in nature. All three murders seemed methodically planned and carried out. The manner in which the body was left, and the use of the votive candle indicate a religious connotation which points to a Visionary motive.

"Most serial killers are white males in their thirties or forties. These killings all indicate a high level of precision and organization. Recent studies have indicated an increased presence of obsessive-compulsive disorder in cases of schizophrenia and forms other mental illness. This may explain why these killers tend to repeat their methods. I agree there seems to be a connection to the medical industry. However, it may just be a coincidence. The killings have a religious context, and I wouldn't rule out the presence of some sort of psychosis. The killer may hear voices and believe it is his mission to kill. At this point, it's my opinion we can eliminate the Power and Control and Hedonistic categories. I'd say these killings are most likely Missionary or Visionary in nature."

"Thank you, Agent Wells," Merchant said. "I'd like you to stay with Detectives Charles and Manson. They'll bring you up to speed on more of the specifics of each one of the murders. We'll be meeting every day until we figure this out. I need to keep Mayor Tecklenburg informed. The pressure to make headway on this will only intensify as this drags on."

~~~~
~~~~

Marcus was at his desk when Adam got back to the bullpen. "How'd the meeting go?"

"Well, I met the FBI profiler. She seemed pretty sharp." Stone then explained the different types of serial killers and Wells' initial thoughts on the case.

"I still say everything points to that Knight guy," Marcus said. "Remember, he's the one who showed signs of OCD in addition to his schizophrenia. Plus, he might be the guy the officers saw around the doctor's office. He wore an army jacket and remember Knight was in the Army."

"Makes sense, but don't forget Tyler Scott tried to enlist in the Army, and his diagnosis seemed more dangerous than Knight's." Adam also mentioned the strange neatness of Bill Bennett's office and Agent Wells' comment on the prevalence of OCD in these kinds of killers. "You got to figure it's probably Knight or Scott, but I still can't shake the feeling there's a chance it might be Bennett or someone else."

~~~~

While Adam and Marcus were working their fentanyl case, Charles Manson was updating Agent Wells on the trio of related murders. They had the murder book for Ann's case, files sent to them from Atlanta, and notes on what little they had gathered so far from the Richardson murder. They first reviewed the similarities between the cases: throats cut, no evidence of sexual assault, candle left at the murder sites. In all three cases, there were no security cameras to record the event
~~~~

They then turned their focus to the details around Charles Knight and Tyler Scott.

"At this point," Claire said, "it seems Knight and Scott are the prime suspects. Knight is currently being treated by Dr. Shaw and Scott is not." She also described the sighting of the man in the army jacket loitering outside of the doctor's office building.

"Interesting," Wells said, "but of course there's the possibility that the killer is someone totally off our radar. Another matter we should be well aware of is that the time between killings is shortening—we may be getting another body soon. On that note, what's being done to protect Dr. Shaw?"

"Patrolmen have been keeping an eye on her office, but with the Richardson murder, we're going to have an officer assigned to her," Claire said.

"Good, now what have you gotten from Knight and Scott so far?"

Manson exchanged looks with his partner and said, "Our forensic psychologist spent some time analyzing their patient files recovered from Ann Stone's practice, and we had an initial meeting with both of them. We didn't get much, but definitely need to get them back in again." It was a weak attempt to cover an obvious mistake in their investigation, and it showed.

Agent Wells tried to keep her dissatisfaction in check, but it was beyond evident. "I suggest you get them in here as soon as possible—as in this afternoon or tomorrow morning."

"We'll have officers bring them in as soon as we can," a red-faced Manson said.

"Good. Now I'd like to spend more time reviewing the files on all three murders. Is there an office I can use?"

Charles Manson collected the files and led Wells to a small conference room. "You can use this as your office while you're here at the station," Claire said.

~~~~

It took several hours to locate Knight and Scott, and they weren't brought into Lockwood until well after 5:00. They arrived separately and were ushered into interview rooms separated by a smaller viewing room. That way both suspects could be observed by simply looking through one of the two windowed mirrors. The interview rooms themselves were rather sparse—approximately 10' by 10' containing a table and chairs, a whiteboard, and obviously the one-way mirror. Adam was in the viewing room along with Merchant, Charles Manson, and Agent Wells.

Both Knight and Scott seemed to be average in height and weight with no physical characteristic that would make them stand out in a crowd. The only interesting aspect of Scott's appearance was a pair of thick, black glasses. He reminded Stone of an older Buddy Holly.

Claire would interview Knight first. Scott, who would be interviewed by Manson, waited alone in the other room.

Before entering the interview room, Claire spent a few moments observing Knight. The most notable thing about him was how normal he looked. He was seated, but it was clear he
~~~~

wasn't a big man—probably around 5' 9" and 150. His light brown hair was on the long side but well kept. He wore faded jeans and a white Tee-shirt. His face and arms were deeply tanned, like a man who spent his days working outdoors. Claire looked for some physical feature or characteristic that would set him apart, but she found none. Charles Knight looked like what might be considered an average man in his mid-thirties. There was a pack of Newports on the table in front of him.

She entered the room and shut the door behind her. "Good evening Mr. Knight. I'm Detective Charles. Can I get you anything before we start?"

"Can I smoke?"

"I'm afraid not, but we appreciate you coming in tonight. I promise we'll get you out of here as soon as we can." Knight frowned but said nothing. "I understand you were a patient of Ann Stone and are currently seeing Dr. Shaw. As you know, Ms. Stone was killed last year, and we're hoping you might be able to help us in our investigation."

Knight seemed nervous and avoided eye contact with Claire. "I don't know anything about that," he said, his voice quiet.

"I appreciate that, Mr. Knight. I just have a few general questions for you. That's all." Knight didn't react. "I understand you had been seeing Ms. Stone for a year or so before her death. Do you ever remember seeing Ms. Stone outside her Savannah Highway office?"

"No. Why would I?"

"No reason. Just curious. And you're now seeing Dr. Shaw, right?"

"Yes."

"How's that working out for you?"

"Okay, I guess."

"How about Dr. Shaw? Have you seen her outside her office?"

"No." He seemed to be growing more nervous.

"Mr. Knight, please relax. We're not saying you had anything to do with Ms. Stone's death. We're just gathering information from some of her old patients." A pitcher of ice water sat on the table. Claire poured a glass and slid it to Knight. "Just a few more questions." He reached for the water and took a sip. Adam, watching through the mirror, noticed he used his right hand.

"I understand you left your job at Parks and Recreation about six months ago," Claire said. "Why'd you decide to leave? It seems like a fun job."

"Too many people," he replied. "It made me nervous."

Claire nodded. "I can understand that. Now you're at Riverview Memorial Park Cemetery. I've been there. It's beautiful. Right next to the Ashley River. What do you do there, Charles?"

"I work for the head groundskeeper."

"How'd you get that job?"

"My minister at church got it for me."

"I take it you go to church a lot."

"Yeah, it makes me feel better."

"I go to church, too. I imagine working outside in the sun all day is pretty tiring. You probably just stay home and relax on the weekends. How about Sunday night? Did you go out that night or just stay home?"

"Stayed home."

"By yourself?"

"Yeah."

Claire spent another fifteen minutes asking mostly non-confrontational questions about his job at the cemetery, his time in the Army, and his therapy sessions with Dr. Shaw. She then thanked him for his help and told him she'd be in touch if she thought of anything else. He was escorted out of the con-ference room, and an officer drove him back to his apartment.

As soon as Knight left, Manson entered Scott's room. "Good evening, Mr. Scott. I'm Detective Manson. I want to thank you for coming down here. This shouldn't take long at all."

Scott was a bit taller and heavier than Knight but appeared to be in good shape. His black hair was tied in a short ponytail and wore a short sleeve blue denim work shirt. A blurry cross tattoo on his forearm looked like it had been inked in prison. He wore a stud earring in his left ear.

Scott had been waiting for about forty-five minutes and was clearly agitated. "Why am I here? I didn't do nothing."

Manson took a seat and tried to calm Scott before his state deteriorated further. "Please relax, Mr. Scott. No one is saying you did anything wrong. I just have a few questions about when you were seeing Ms. Ann Stone. My partner and I are working the case and are talking to all the people she was seeing at the time she died. Just general background information. That's all." Manson poured a glass of ice water and passed it to Scott. "Here you go. I was wondering why you decided not to see Dr. Shaw after Ms. Stone died. I understand she took over her practice."

Scott took the water with his right hand and drank. "Well, nothing about that is any of your business. That's medical stuff, and the government says it's private. I didn't have anything to do with Stone's murder. You can't pin that shit on me. Maybe I should get a lawyer in here."

"Mr. Scott, this is just routine. No one thinks you had anything to do with what happened to Ms. Stone. Please, just take it easy and relax. And I know you'd want to help us find who did this terrible thing, right?"

That seemed to put him somewhat more at ease. "Yeah, sure. But I had nothing to do with it."

"We know that. I know you're not working at the airport anymore. Where are you now?"

"BK Lawn Service. Cutting lawns and stuff."

Matt smiled and made a gesture at the four walls of the room. "I'm stuck inside here most of the time and don't get a chance to get out in the sun much. Doesn't sound so bad to me. Do you like it?"

"It's fine."

"You know, I was wondering, when you were seeing Ms. Stone, did you ever happen to see her outside her Savannah Highway office? That's where you saw her, right?"

"Yeah. No. I mean I only saw her in the office."

"And how are you getting along these days, now that you're no longer in therapy?"

"I'm fine." Manson let the silence build, trying to compel Scott to continue. "I want to get out of here," Scott finally said. "I didn't do anything, and you got no right to keep me here."

"Sure, Tyler. I just have a quick question about Sunday night. Do you happen to remember where you were?"

Scott tensed up. "No. Watched TV."

Manson tried a few more questions, but it was obvious Scott was done talking and Manson had no choice but to let him go. An officer drove Scott back to his Brentwood apartment, and Manson joined everyone in the observation room.

"Well, that was a bust," Manson said.

"Not really," Agent Wells offered. "It's clear they're both hiding something, and now they're both shaken up. They know the police are interested in them. If they're connected to these killings, who knows what they may do now, perhaps something that tips their hand." She turned to Merchant. "I suggest you put an officer on each of them."

"The department's been worn thin with all the pressure from the Richardson murder, and it's only going to get worse. But I'm sure the chief will authorize surveillance."

"There's something else I don't get," Manson said. "How could Knight and Scott afford to be seeing a psychologist? Both their jobs were probably close to minimum wage."

Agent Wells said, "I read where Charles Knight was in the Army, so I'm sure the VA covered the cost for him. And I imagine Medicaid paid for Scott."

"I don't know if anyone else noticed," Adam said, "but both Knight and Scott look to be right-handed."

"Most people are," Agent Wells reminded him. But she made a note.

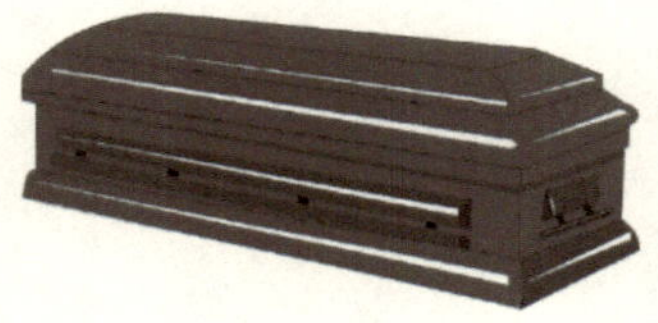

# CHAPTER SEVENTEEN
### Friday, March 29

WORK ON BOTH the fentanyl and Richardson cases was intense for the balance of the week with both Adam and Marcus working well into the night. Tracy agreed to spend those nights at Adam's apartment to take care of Piper. In addition to providing protection for Kate Shaw, Merchant was able to get authorization to have officers surveil both Knight and Scott.

By Friday afternoon, everyone was dragging. They'd been consumed by the investigations. "Hey Marcus, are you and Makayla doing anything tonight?" Adam questioned.

"Nope."

"I haven't spent much time with Piper, and I'm taking her and Tracy to Low Tide tonight for some R&R. Why don't you and the wife join us?"

"That's the best offer I've had so far. I'll check with Makayla, but I'm sure she'll be up for it. What time?"

"The place fills up Fridays. How about 6:00 or so?"

"That'll work. I could sure use a break."

Low Tide Brewery is one of a growing number of family-oriented private craft beer breweries popping up across the country. It's located down Maybank Highway just a few miles from Adam's apartment. The inside of the place had a rustic feel to it with several large flat screen TVs and a long bar offering a variety of beers that were brewed in the large stainless-steel vats right there on the premises. *Chicken Fats*, one of Adam's favorite food trucks, was parked on the grounds. It offered an excellent selection of chicken sandwiches and sides.

It was a beautiful spring evening with clear skies and temperatures in the upper sixties. Adam, Tracy, and Piper arrived early and commandeered one of the few remaining outside picnic tables. Low Tide was dog friendly, and they'd brought Max who was taking in all the sights and smells of the place. Marcus, or "Uncle Marcus" as Piper called him, showed up with Makayla around 6:30.

Adam put his arm around Marcus' huge shoulders and said, "Come on, buddy, first round is on me." One of the TVs inside the bar showed a list of all the various kinds of beers available with names like; *Hoppy Ending Pale Ale, Blind Pig IPA,* and *Brew Free! Or Die! IPA.*

"Christ," Marcus said, "what ever happened to good old Bud Lite, Coors, or Iron City?"

"Modern times, my friend," Adam said with a smile. They ordered their beers and a lemonade for Piper and Tracy and returned to the picnic table. A half hour and another round of beers later, they ordered food.

It was about 7:30, and they'd just finished eating when Marcus felt his cell vibrate. As he covered his left ear and listened, his grin quickly vanished. "When?" he said, "All right." He stood and motioned Adam to join him away from the table.

Adam read the concern on his partner's face. "What was that all about?"

"That was the officer assigned to review the daily recordings from the seed microphone at the art gallery. He was just getting around to listen to it, and the mics picked up a conversation between Alvarez and Davis about a delivery of a 'China Girl' coming in on a ship."

China Girl is the street name for heroin dusted with fentanyl. Or at least one of them—there seemed to be a new nickname for the deadly mixture every week: Apache, China White, Goodfella, Jackpot, Tango. Adam sometimes struggled to keep them all straight.

"The damned thing worked," Adam said. "We need to get down to the station and listen to that tape."

"No doubt."

They returned to the table and Marcus broke the news. "Listen. I'm sorry, folks, but Adam and I need to get downtown." He pulled out his keys and gave them to Makayla.

"Honey, I'll ride with Adam. Can you drop off Tracy and Piper?"

They'd been married long enough for Makayla not to question the *whys* and *whens* of his job. She gave her husband a hug and said, "Sure. Call me and let me know when you'll be home."

Tracy and Piper were also concerned but, like Makayla, knew calls like this were part of police work.

Another apology and a round of hugs, and Adam and Marcus headed across the Connector to Lockwood. Marcus had assigned the task of reviewing the daily recordings to a rookie named Billy Spence, who looked like a junior in high school. But he was eager, and you had to be eager to sift through that much audio and not miss a thing. Spence had downloaded the recording and cued it up to the beginning of the conversation between Alvarez and Davis. Marcus thanked him and told him they'd take it from here.

Marcus hit play, and the recording started.

> **Alvarez**: *Interesting painting.*
> **Davis**: *Yeah.*
> **Alvarez**: *I'm not sure I understand it, but I like the colors.*
> **Davis**: *Yeah.*
> **Alvarez**: (pause) *The China Girl's coming in.*
> **Davis**: *When?*

**Alvarez**: *It's on a small bulk cargo ship named the* Orion. *Coming into North Charleston Terminal next Tuesday.*

**Davis**: *All right.*

**Alvarez**: *Three crew members on the ship are working for us. They got the merchandise. I've arranged to have my people pick them up at the terminal and drive them to this address.*

**Davis**: (pause) *I know the place.*

**Alvarez**: *Good. The exchange will be made there. Have your people ready. You'll be advised about an hour before they arrive at the warehouse.*

**Davis**: *Okay. I'll take care of it.*

**Alvarez**: *I'm going now. Wait five minutes before you leave.*

Marcus smiled. "All right, so now we know who's transporting the drugs. This almost feels too easy. Would have been nice if they'd gone the extra mile and told us where it's going, but at least they gave us enough head's up to get Chito Walker's SWAT team organized."

Marcus slapped Adam on his back. "We hit pay dirt, partner!"

"Damn right! And we know this is a big shipment if Alvarez is involved."

Despite the late hour, Marcus got ahold of Ed Merchant, and he said they'd get together Saturday afternoon with Frank Butler and Chito Walker to start planning the operation. There wasn't much more to do that night, so Adam dropped off Marcus at his place and headed home.

~~~~

The following afternoon, Ed merchant, Chito Walker, along with North Charleston's Terminal Manager, Frank Butler, met up with them to plan the details of the operation which would commence this coming Tuesday afternoon. Merchant got the meeting started by asking Adam and Marcus to bring everyone up to speed. He then asked Frank Butler to review the security in place at the North Charleston Terminal.

"Well," Butler began, "we do what we can, but it's almost impossible to check more than a small percentage of the cargo at our facilities. We use scanners and police dogs to check for narcotics and explosives, but it's impossible to vet everything coming in and going out. Of course, everything runs a lot smoother when we know what we're looking for."

"Actually," Merchant said, "in this case we want you to make sure the three crewmembers on the Orion aren't checked. We need them to leave the terminal, so we can follow them to wherever the drug transfer is going to be made. That way we can take down more of the operation."

"Got it," Butler said. "Marcus said the batch of heroin coming in has probably been treated with fentanyl. What street value are we looking at with this stuff?"

"A kilo of heroin sells for about $60,000," Marcus said. "That can go up to a few hundred thousand dollars when it's
~~~~

diluted and sold by the gram. But because of fentanyl's potency, it's much easier to cut. This can increase the dealer's profits up to ten or more times. Fentanyl's bad shit. A speck the size of a few grains of sand can be deadly."

They spent the next hour hashing out the plan for what they'd deemed Operation Orion. Merchant knew he'd have to bring in the FBI and DEA on the SWAT raid but wanted to organize Operation Orion himself. He also knew the Feds, especially the FBI, played tug-of-war with local law enforcement. But this was his town and his turf. No matter what the Feds thought, he was determined to call the shots on this game.

<center>~~~~</center>

When Adam got back home, Piper, Tracy, and Max were parked in front of the TV. He wasn't about to let them spend another night cooped up in the apartment. He clapped his hands and said, "Come on you two, let's take Max to the dog park. It's a beautiful day! Plus, we never got to finish our night out last night. What do you say we go to the park and then get a bite to eat on the way home?"

As soon as Max heard the word, *park*, he was up—his tail doing double time. Tracy laughed, "Looks like Max is up for it! You guys go ahead, I need to get home and get some work done."

"All right, Piper", Adam said, "how about some good old father/daughter bonding?"

Piper rolled her eyes. "Sure, Dad. Whatever."

A few minutes later, Piper and Max were in the car, and Adam made the ten-minute drive to the dog park. As soon as they were through the gated opening, Piper removed Max's leash, and he dashed off to commiserate with the fifteen or twenty other dogs roaming the grass-covered grounds. Piper wandered off by herself. There were several wooden picnic tables throughout the park, and Adam headed to one and joined several folks watching the animals romp and play together. About five minutes later, Max showed up with a tennis ball in his mouth.

"Hey, boy, where'd you get the ball?" He took the ball from Max's mouth and stood up. His eyes moved in a steady arc around the park until he saw a woman about fifty yards away waving to him. She was tall with light blond hair and a nice smile. It was hard to tell from this distance, but she looked to be in her mid-thirties. She seemed attractive but not in a way that drew undue attention to her. He pointed to the tennis ball, and she nodded and started to walk over. Adam met her about halfway. "Sorry. Looks like my dog is a thief."

"Oh, don't worry," the woman replied, "I'm still trying to get my dog to even chase the darn thing." Just as she finished speaking, a black and white Border Collie mix showed up with Max right behind her. The two dogs did their traditional nose to butt circle dance—the canine version of "Hi there, what's your name?"

Adam reached down and ruffled the Collie's neck. "What's her name?"

The woman smiled. "That's Sugar. She's a Border Collie plus some other breeds thrown in. We got her at the shelter on Folly Road."

Adam pointed to Max. "That's where we got Max. He's also a mix. There's definitely Lab in there with a sprinkling of who knows what else. It looks like they like each other." He held his hand out and said, "I'm Adam."

She shook his hand. "Nice to meet you, Adam. I'm Lisa. Do you come here often?"

Adam had to smile and thought to himself, *Do you come here often? Reminds me of one of the bar lines I used to use in college.* "Yep, at least once a week. More if we can." Adam looked around the park. "My daughter, Piper, is around here somewhere."

"Me, too. I mean I'm also here with my daughter." Lisa pointed off toward the small lake. "Actually, she's over there in the red sweatshirt."

The sun was sinking low in the sky. Haloed by the fading light, Adam had to shield his eyes when he glanced over toward where Lisa was pointing. He saw Piper talking to the girl in the red sweatshirt. "It looks like she's talking to my daughter. Maybe they know each other. Where does your daughter go to school?"

"Charleston Collegiate. She's in the eighth grade."

"How about that," Adam said, "That's where Piper goes. Looks like they're classmates!" He called out to Piper, and she waved back. Piper said something to her friend, and they jogged over to where Adam and Lisa were standing.

"Hey, Dad, I didn't know you knew Chloe's mom."

"No, sweetheart, we just met."

"Adam," Lisa quickly said, "this is my daughter, Chloe."

"Hi, Mrs. White," Piper said, and both girls dashed off toward the lake with Sugar and Max chasing after them.

Lisa laughed. "I remember when I had that much energy!"

"Your daughter seems like a great kid," Adam said, "You and your husband must be very proud."

Lisa White was quiet for a moment and then said, "I'm very proud of her and while I know her dad is too, Chloe and I are on our own. Chloe's dad and I split about ten years ago. He's out in California, but he sees Chloe as much as he can."

"I'm sorry, I didn't mean to pry."

"No, not at all. We actually get along better now than when we were married. Plus, I'm thankful he's still part of Chloe's life."

They talked for another fifteen minutes with Adam learning Lisa worked at MUSC as a surgical nurse and lived with Chloe on James Island. Her husband is an attorney and paid for Chloe's tuition at Charleston Collegiate—which was a hefty $20,000 plus a year. Adam told Lisa that his wife, Ann, had passed away but didn't go into any details. Even though Lisa had never met Adam, she remembered the murder of Ann Stone and how it had rocked Charleston Collegiate.

Adam felt comfortable around her, and their conversation flowed easily. She seemed open and down to earth, with a smile that was both contagious and disarming.

When Piper and Chloe returned, Piper said, "Dad, I told Chloe we're going to get something to eat on the way home. Can Chloe and her mom come with us?"

Chloe chimed in, "Please, Mom. It's Saturday, and we've got nothing else to do."

"No, dear, I'm sure they have plans, and we don't want to impose."

Both Piper and Chloe looked at Adam and he said, "We're just going to grab a quick bite—nothing special. You're more than welcome to join us. We can go to Low Tide and take the dogs with us. I don't know what food truck is there, but I'm sure it's good."

"Are you sure?" Lisa said.

"Absolutely."

"Okay. That's very nice of you."

"Great, we'll meet you guys there."

They all arrived at the brewery, dogs in tow, fifteen minutes later. It was still early, and they had no trouble finding a table outside next to the *Easy Slider* food truck. "What can I get everyone to drink?" Adam asked.

The kids ordered lemonade, and Lisa said, "Whatever you're having, Adam."

"How about an IPA?"

"Sounds great. And maybe some water for the pups?" she added.

Adam returned with the drinks and they settled in. A few orders of turkey and cheeseburger sliders later, and they were all full. It was an enjoyable evening, and Lisa insisted on paying half the bill. On the way home, Adam thought to himself what a nice evening it was. Ann had been gone for over a year, and he missed her deeply. With his work and taking care of Piper, he'd never given much thought about seeing anyone else. Friends had made a few attempts at introductions, but he showed no interest, and their efforts eventually stopped.

As they drove into the apartment complex, Piper surprised him by saying, "You know, Dad, I think it's time you started to date. I know Mom would want you to."

"Whoa there! What brought that on?"

"Mrs. White is really nice, and Chloe and I decided you two should see each other again."

"Slow down, sweetheart! Even if I wanted to—and I'm not saying I do—Mrs. White would have something to say about that."

"Don't worry about that. Chloe's going to tell her she should go out with you."

Adam started to laugh. "So, you two are matchmakers now!"

"Come on, Dad. You should do this! All you do is work."

"We'll see, honey. We'll see." But he had to admit to himself that the thought of spending more time with Lisa White was somewhat intriguing. He'd only just met her, but they say you often finds special things when you're not looking for something special. He had definitely felt relaxed around her. Most people Adam met for the first time socially tended to talk mostly about themselves, and Adam had to admit he was, at times, guilty as charged. Lisa, on the other hand, seemed sincerely interested in him—always leading the conversation away from herself and toward one of the kids or him. She had a positive air about her, and Adam hadn't had a whole lot of "positive" in his life lately.

He actually felt guilty for even considering thoughts of seeing another woman. But he knew Ann would have wanted him to move on with his life. With Ann gone now, Piper had to rely on Tracy for adult female support in her life. Maybe seeing someone like Lisa would be good for Piper. He had to laugh when he realized that he was actually just trying to talk himself into the whole thing!

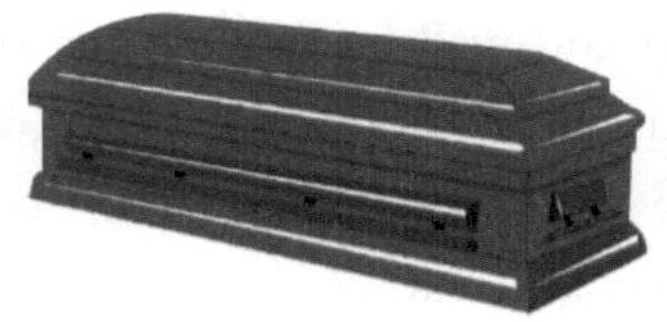

# CHAPTER EIGHTEEN

Sunday, March 31

ADAM WAS UP early Sunday morning. The evening with Lisa White had been enjoyable, but the recent murders of Camila Hanson and Sally Richardson quickly brought him back to reality. Piper would be sleeping in, and Merchant's meeting with FBI and DEA agents wasn't scheduled until noon. No way was Adam going to sit around the apartment all morning. He'd remembered how defensive and evasive both Knight and Scott had been when they were interrogated—especially Tyler Scott.

A half hour later, Adam was sitting in his Charger outside Scott's Brentwood apartment. A short time later, he watched

Scott leave his apartment and drive away in an old Dodge Neon. He waited five minutes before getting out of the Charger and approaching the apartment—a small two-story structure with four apartments. The mail slot inside the doorway indicated Scott lived in apartment 2C. Adam slipped on crime scene gloves and took less than sixty seconds to pick the lock.

Once inside, Adam closed and locked the door behind him. The small two room apartment was sparsely furnished but looked to be clean and well kept. He wasn't sure exactly what he was looking for, but he certainly knew where and how to case the place. He systematically began going through kitchen appliances, drawers, and cabinets careful not to disturb their contents. He did the same in the bathroom and bedroom. The bathroom cabinet was replete with pill bottles in addition to basic toiletries. A well-worn Bible and rosary were on one of the nightstands and a few soldier of fortune-type magazines on the other. Several framed illustrations of Jesus hung on the walls. The dresser held nothing out of the ordinary, but when Adam was going through the closet, he froze. Hanging in the back was a well-worn camouflaged army jacket. He took out his cell and snapped a picture. There were a few cardboard boxes stacked in the corner of the closet, but they held nothing that seemed incriminating. Not wanting to push his luck, he double-checked that everything was as he found it and quickly left the apartment. He sat for a few minutes in his car contemplating what he'd discovered. He thought about the mysterious man in the army jacket that he'd chased outside of Shaw's office building. The only thing of consequence in his search was the discovery of the army jacket. It was far from something that would ID Scott as the killer, but it did increase the likelihood he might have been involved. He couldn't share this discovery because the way he discovered it was obviously out of bounds.

He arrived at Lockwood shortly before FBI's Jim Strickland and DEA's Bob Francis. They'd been involved with previous drug cases in Charleston, and with the exception of the latest intel on the Orion, they were up to speed on the case.

Merchant began, "We don't know the identities of the three deckhands that will be transporting the drugs off the Orion, but based on the recorded conversation, we know someone from the East Side Posse will pick them up. The Orion's safety procedures require a minimum of six general deck personnel. All non-terminal employees are picked up and dropped off at the terminal visitor's entry gate on Remount Road. We'll have several teams familiar with the Posse covertly stationed at that gate.

"We'll also have an undercover officer at the exit ramp of the Orion. He'll be relaying descriptions of men leaving the ship to the officers stationed at the gate. They'll be in a position to follow any crew members being picked up there."

He looked at agents Strickland and Francis. "You two and your people will be with us and Chito Walker's SWAT Team at the North Charleston Police Station off East Montague. We'll deploy after we know where the drugs are headed. Chito, go ahead an outline your assault plans."

"Thanks, Ed. As soon as the drop location is identified, SWAT Team One will seal off the area and secure the perimeter. Flash bang grenades and tear gas will be used prior to Team Two breaching the building and entering the premises. Once the situation is neutralized, you can bring your agents in."

The discussion lasted another half hour, and as it wrapped, Merchant offered some final points. "We will rendezvous at North Charleston station Tuesday no later than 3:30. The terminal's chief security officer will make sure the Orion crewmembers don't leave before 5:00 and are not stopped by security. I'll let you all know if the timing changes on any of this."

~~~~

Adam had settled onto his living room couch for the afternoon when he noticed—through half-closed eyes—that Piper was casting him a succession of furtive glances, punctuated by furious texting.

"Let's take Max to the dog park," Piper said loud enough for Max to hear. Hearing the word, "park," Max was up, tail wagging, obviously excited for another adventure.

Tracy grinned and shook her head, "Well, I guess we don't have a choice now." They all climbed into the Charger and headed off to the park. Once inside the park, Max took off followed by Piper. Adam and Tracy relaxed on one of the picnic tables—taking in the cool but pleasant afternoon. There was a slight breeze with puffy white clouds floating across a deep blue Charleston sky. About ten minutes later, Adam glanced toward the entrance and saw Chloe, her mother, and their dog, Sugar, walk through the gate. Piper met them there,
~~~~

and they all walked over to the picnic table where Adam and Tracy were seated.

When they reached the picnic table, Piper said, "Dad, look who showed up!"

Lisa shrugged her shoulders, smiled, and said, "Well, Adam Stone, fancy meeting *you* here."

Adam looked at Piper and Chloe and said, "Hi, Lisa, what a coincidence."

As soon as he introduced Tracy to Lisa and Chloe, Piper said, "Come on, Granny, I want to show you something." Tracy, Piper, Chloe, and the dogs headed off leaving Adam and Lisa alone.

After an awkward moment, they both broke out laughing. "I get the feeling this was somehow planned," Lisa said.

"I think you're right. I sense a plot developing here."

"I'm sorry, Adam. I didn't know you'd be here. But I think you're right. Chloe and Piper have obviously been working on getting us together again."

"Well," Adam said with a smile, "I can't say I'm disappointed. I had fun last night."

"I don't get out much, and it was fun for me, too."

"You know, Lisa, our girls must have spent a lot of time organizing this little get together. I don't think we should disappoint them. If you're not busy, would you like to go out sometime?"

"I'd like that, Adam. But please don't feel obligated because of the girls."

"Not at all. I have to admit that I've been hoping I'd see you again. There's a new restaurant that opened up on Maybank called the Royal Tern, and it's supposed to be pretty good. How about Saturday evening? That is, if you're not busy."

"That would be great."

They talked for a few more minutes until Piper, Chloe, and Tracy returned with the dogs. Adam looked serious when he said, "Now, girls, Ms. White and I have something to ask you two." The girls frowned. "We were wondering if you two would have a problem if the two of us went out to dinner together."

Piper and Chloe gave each other a High Five. Adam quickly glanced at Tracy for her reaction. It had been over a year since she'd lost her only child. It had been a year of pain and frustration. The pain would never dissipate, but for the sake of Piper and Adam, it was time to move on. She gave a slight nod of approval.

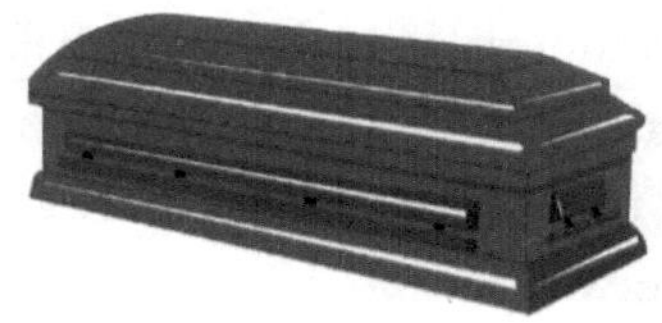

# CHAPTER NINETEEN

Tuesday, April 2

AS PLANNED, AN undercover officer was stationed at the Orion on Tuesday afternoon, additional officers had gathered at the Remount terminal exit. SWAT Teams along with FBI and DEA personnel were assembled at the North Charleston station. Now it was a waiting game.

Shortly after 5:00 that afternoon, men began leaving the Orion. The first few left by themselves followed by a pair of sailors. Then, after a watchful stretch that seemed longer than it was, the officer stationed at the Orion radioed that a group of three crewmembers was leaving the ship with backpacks.

The three arrived at the gate five minutes later and got into a black Suburban. Two of the undercover police cars followed the Suburban down Remount to Rt. 52. The officers were somewhat surprised when the SUV turned away from downtown Charleston and toward Goose Creek. The trailing police cars were in constant contact with Merchant and the personnel at the North Charleston Police Station. Chito Walker's SWAT teams were on Rt. 52, as well, not far behind.

Twenty-five minutes later, the Suburban turned onto Old Town Road. Shortly after that, it pulled into a gravel driveway leading to a small prefab steel building in a forested, secluded area with only one way in and out. A detective from the first trailing car approached on foot. Crouching behind a stand of trees, he identified four vehicles parked outside the building. He couldn't locate the Suburban and assumed it had entered the warehouse.

Timing was critical. As soon as the location was reconnoitered, Walker issued deployment instructions based on the location and layout of the warehouse. Team One took a position around the perimeter, and Team Two proceeded toward the driveway using trees as cover. The tactical armored SWAT vehicles were parked fifty yards from the entrance. The officers were armed with Benelli M1 shotguns, 9mm HK MP5 assault rifles, and Sig Sauer 9mm pistols, in addition to protective eyewear and gas masks.

With everyone in position, Merchant nodded to Chito, and the assault commenced. Led by an officer carrying a 38-pound Blackhawk battering ram, Team Two positioned itself outside the warehouse's main entrance. On command, the officer breached the door on his first attempt. Two flash-bang grenades, designed to disorient, exploded a few seconds later with 170–180 decibels and a blinding flash. The grenades were followed by a teargas canister and a stream of officers snaking in single file, minimizing the number of team members presenting an open target.

The entire raid was completed in less than three minutes. Odell Davis along with eight other suspects were apprehended without a single shot fired. Merchant, Stone, Williams and the Feds entered as the tear gas dissipated. The Orion crew-members' backpacks contained a total of thirty kilos of fentanyl-dusted heroin. The heroin, two suitcases containing approximately $3 million in cash, and a variety of weapons were confiscated in the raid. The only disappointment was that Miguel Alvarez was not inside. When FBI agents showed up with a warrant at the Hilton, Alvarez was long gone.

The balance of the week was hectic for Adam and Marcus, as they worked to tie up loose ends on Operation Orion. A substantial amount of intel was gathered on the Sinaloa Cartel, and a major blow was dealt to the East Side Posse's drug activities. A press conference was televised with the mayor, police chief, FBI, and DEA agents displaying the bounty seized in the raid. The news gathered intense local coverage and was soon picked up nationally.

It was late Friday afternoon, and Adam and Marcus were back in the bullpen finishing up paperwork when a uniform approached and said, "Chief Taylor wants you guys in his office."

Marcus shrugged. "What's up with that?"

Taylor was at his desk looking somber when they walked in. He pointed at the chairs in front of his desk. "Sit. I just got off the phone with the mayor—he's not happy with you two."

"What the hell's his problem?" Marcus said. "Holy shit, Chief, we just took down a major drug ring—not to mention three million in cash recovered."

"He said you didn't capture Alvarez!"

They were both out of their seats. "Jesus Christ," Adam said. "You have to be fu ..."

But before he could say another word, Taylor broke out laughing. "Sit down, detectives. I'm just messing with you. This has been a hell of an accomplishment for the department, and we deserve to enjoy it. But we can't forget we've still got a serial killer out there." He then opened his bottom desk drawer and removed three glasses and a fifth of Maker's Mark. He poured shots and pushed two across the desk. "One hell of a job, detectives!" The three men tapped their glasses together and downed the whiskey. As Adam put down the shot glass, his only thought was the fact that Ann's killer was still out there somewhere.

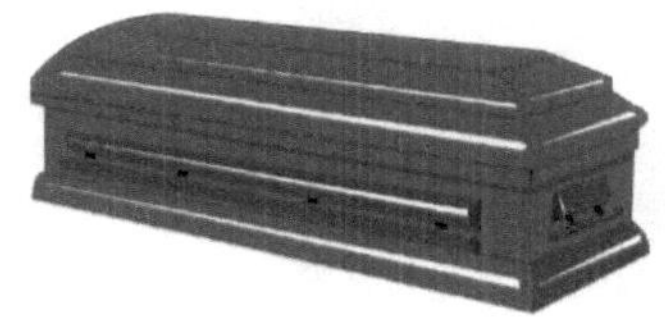

# CHAPTER TWENTY

Saturday, April 6

*KATE SHAW PULLED* into her garage on Saturday afternoon, waved off the police officer that had followed her back from her office, and entered her West Ashley house. She'd called the officer earlier that morning letting him know she needed a few hours at her office to catch up on paperwork.

She shut the front door and called out to her cat. "Freud, I'm home." She hung up her jacket and walked into the kitchen. Freud was waiting next to his bowl. "Lunch is served," she said, the bowl clinking with kibble. She freshened his water and headed into her bedroom to change.

Before she could open the closet, a savage blow dropped her to her knees. Her mind flashed white light and exploded into a thousand dancing *diamonds. She was dazed when an arm encircled her neck and pushed her head forward. Within ten seconds she lost consciousness.*

*The military chokehold was released, and 10 ml of propofol was injected into her neck. She was gently placed on the bed, and for the next hour, her condo was cleaned, and the living room furniture rearranged. Shaw's vitals were periodically checked, an injection repeated when necessary to maintain her sedation. It was around 3:00 that afternoon when she was carried into the garage and placed in the front seat of her car. A candle was lit.*

~~~~

The reservation for their dinner at the Royal Tern was set for 6:30. Dressed and ready at 5:30, Adam had to admit to himself that he was feeling a little nervous about tonight. He decided to take Max for a quick walk before he left to pick up Lisa. He'd been married to Ann for over fourteen years, and they'd dated for a year before getting hitched. He looked at Max and said, "Well, Max, I hope I remember how to do this dating thing."

Tracy arrived a few minutes later and Adam said, "Thanks for watching Piper, I promise I won't be out late."

"Pshaw, Adam. You stay out as long as you want. I think Ms. White is sweet, and both of you deserve to have some adult time. You know; no dogs, no daughters, no grandma. Seriously, I think it's nice you're getting out, and I'm glad it's with someone like Ms. White."

Adam was still a bit concerned Tracy wouldn't be onboard with him going on a date, but she did seem all right with it.
~~~~

Lisa's house was a short ten-minute drive from the apartment, and Adam pulled into her driveway at a few minutes before 6:00. He knocked on the front door, and Chloe opened it. "Hi, Mr. Stone. Mom's upstairs. She's been up there a long time." Chloe sighed, "I think she's nervous. You know she hasn't been with a man for a long time."

Adam suppressed a smile. After shutting the front door, he turned around and saw Lisa coming down the stairs. She had a casual but alluring look—wearing a light gray cashmere sweater and form-fitting stone washed jeans tucked into a pair of black leather ankle boots. Her light blond hair fell loosely over her shoulders, and a simple silver cross hung around her neck. She was smiling and her eyes seemed as blue as a summer's sky.

"Hi, Adam."

"Hi, Lisa. You look great." He glanced at Chloe who was definitely enjoying the whole scene.

"Now, Chloe, Jennifer will be here soon to sit for you tonight."

"Geez, Mom, I'm almost thirteen! I don't need a babysitter."

"I know, dear. I just feel better if someone is with you. I left money on the kitchen counter, so go ahead and order a pizza. We won't be late, and I've got my phone, so you can call me if you need to."

Chloe rolled her eyes. "I'll be fine, Mom. Have fun."

The restaurant was packed, and after a ten-minute wait, they were seated. Their waiter rattled off the specials and took their drink order—a pinot noir for Adam and a sauvignon blanc for Lisa. They chatted for a few minutes until the waiter brought their wine.

Adam raised his glass and said, "Let's toast to something."

Lisa smiled, "Okay, what should we toast to?"

Adam thought a moment, "How about here's to new beginnings?"

They touched glasses and Lisa said, "New beginnings. I like that."

Their meals were excellent, and their conversation pleasant. It hopscotched between their girls and work. Adam was fascinated with Lisa's job as a surgical nurse, and Lisa viewed his detective work with the same level of interest. They were both surprisingly comfortable and felt as if they'd known each other for longer than only a few days. Eventually, talk got around to their previous marriages.

"I think is great that Chloe's father is still involved in her life," Adam said.

"I have to admit he's a good dad—as much as he can be living all the way across the country. We were only married or a few years before we split. We were just too young to really know what we were doing. But still, we have Chloe, and that made the whole thing worthwhile."

"I know what you mean. I'd be lost without Piper. I think we both lucked out on that score." They ordered another glass of wine, and the conversation wandered from their life growing up, to school, and to their likes and dislikes—interesting but safe territory.

Despite how comfortable he felt around Lisa; Adam was not ready to open up about Ann. Since her death, he'd put up a good front. People often commented on how strong he'd been since the tragedy, but the truth was that he'd merely created a façade … a protective cocoon, like he'd hung a no trespassing sign on his emotions.

It took almost a year before he realized what he was doing—not only to himself but, more importantly, what he had been doing to Piper and Tracy. They were the strong ones. They were the ones who saved him. It wasn't as if he'd accepted Ann's death. He doubted he ever would. But at least he was coming to terms with it and was able to consider the future.

The Royal Tern did itself proud with Lisa ordering the grilled salmon and Adam the blackened swordfish. Their meals were topped off with a shared crème brûlée and two cups of espresso. Leaving the restaurant, Adam suggested they stop by a small park located next to the Stono River just off the Johns Island Connector.

It was a beautiful evening, and the air was as cool and fresh as a dinner mint. After a short walk in the park, they found a stone bench by the edge of the river and sat there enjoying the last rays of the setting sun. The sky was ablaze with crimson-colored shafts of light turning the last remnants of clouds a golden-yellow. The fading light played off the water mirroring the glow of the day's end. A cabin cruiser slowly made its way south heading toward the ocean and parts unknown. It wasn't a perfect sunset, but it was damn close.

As the sun fell below the horizon, the sky turned a soft gray, and the evening grew cooler. A breeze, carrying the scent of the sea, sent ripples across the surface of the water, and the high-pitched sound of seagulls could be heard as dusk fell on the Stono. Lisa shivered. Despite not wanting to lose the moment, Adam whispered, "You're cold. We should get back to the car."

"No, it's so beautiful. We can sit a little longer." She leaned into Adam, and he put his arm around her. They sat together quietly for some time savoring the sights and sounds as night folded over them.

After a while, Adam could feel Lisa shivering. "Come on, let's get you warmed up." They walked back to the car arm in arm. A few minutes after leaving the park, Adam pulled into Lisa's driveway and turned off the car. "You know," he began, "I was at the school today watching Piper's soccer game, and Nancy Parker knew we were going out tonight."

Lisa chuckled, "Why does that not surprise me? It doesn't bother me, though. How about you?"

"No, not really," Adam said and then smiled, "Looks like all the mothers are going to be talking about us."

Lisa moved closer to Adam. "Well, maybe we should give them something to talk about." She put her hand on his cheek and gave him a soft kiss.

"I agree," and he was about to return the kiss when his cell rang.

"Maybe you should get that. It might be Piper," Lisa whispered.

"How's that for poor timing?" he groaned and pulled out his cell. It was Marcus. "Sorry, Lisa. I need to take this." He put the phone to his ear. "What's up, partner?" He listened for a moment as Marcus gave him the news of Kate Shaw's murder. "All right, I'm on my way."

Lisa's voice was filled with concern, "Adam, what is it?"

"There's been a murder. I need to get down to the station."

"Of course."

She got out of the car, and Adam lowered the passenger window. "Listen, tonight was perfect. I'll call you."

"Yes, it felt right. Please be safe and call me when you can. Please, just call me."

# CHAPTER TWENTY-ONE
### Saturday, April 6

ADAM WALKED INTO the bullpen and found it alive with activity. A detective yelled at him across the room. "Hey Stone, Williams is up in the Kennels. They want you up there!"

He took the stairs two at a time. Marcus, Merchant, Charles, a group of other detectives and Agent Wells were gathered around a desk, deep in conversation. Merchant saw Adam and waved him over.

Merchant's face was drawn and tired. Crow's feet had taken up permanent residence in the corner of his eyes, and frown lines were embedded deep in his forehead.

"What have we've got?" Adam asked.

"Not much so far," Merchant said, "but the murder matches the Richardson killing."

"And Ann's," Adam said, more to himself than the group.

"I'm afraid so, Adam. Manson's still out at the scene with CSI." He turned to Claire Charles. "Claire, tell Adam what we have so far."

"The department got a 911 call around 8:00 this evening from a friend of Shaw's named Judy Weaver. Weaver said they'd planned on watching a movie at Shaw's, but when she arrived, no one answered the door. She called Shaw, got no answer, and then let herself in—the door was unlocked. She checked all the rooms and then looked in the garage. That's where she found Dr. Shaw, in her passenger's seat, throat cut."

"And there was a candle." Adam said, more statement than question.

"Yeah. On the dashboard."

"I know you've all got your own cases," Merchant said, "but, as much as you can, I need you to put them on the back burner. This is priority number one. We've got a serial killer on our hands."

Somehow the fact got out that a candle was found at the murder scenes, and the media was now referring to the murders as "The Candle Killings."

"It's only going to get worse. The FBI is already in on this. I know they can be a pain in the ass, but I need you all to park your egos and work with them. We need all the help we can get. Chief Taylor's going to schedule another press conference tomorrow. The news that there may be a serial killer in our town is like throwing chum in the water. The shit's going to hit the fan, and I want us as prepared as possible when it starts to fly.

"Charles and Manson are working the Stone and Richardson cases—in addition to keeping up with the ongoing investigation out of Atlanta. They'll be point on this one, too. We work nonstop until this is solved. All personnel leaves, vacations, and whatever are cancelled as of now. I want Charles Knight and Tyler Scott back in here ASAP. We got virtually nothing the last time they were questioned. We're getting warrants to search their apartments while they're here. Agent Wells, I'd like you to work with Charles and Manson during the interrogations. Detective Williams, you'll be our interface with the other police departments in and around Charleston. It's critical that we keep them informed and control what information is given to the public. The news media is going to be all over this. I want all inquiries directed to my office. All right then, I want everyone working your contacts. Call in your markers."

As the conference room emptied, Merchant called out to Adam. "Listen," he said when the room had cleared, "I know I initially had to keep you on the sidelines. The hell with that now. We need you. You're to work closely with Agent Wells. You know our city and its players, so take what she gives you and see how it plays on the street. I also want you with her and Charles Manson when they interrogate Knight and Scott."

"Thanks Ed, I appreciate that." He thought to himself; *It's about fucking time!*

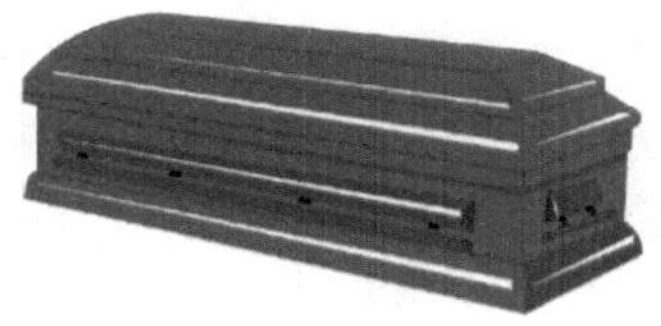

# **CHAPTER TWENTY-TWO**

Sunday, April 7

ADAM HADN'T TOLD Tracy that Kate Shaw was the murder victim or the fact that the killing was a mirror image of Ann's murder. He knew it would come out when it hit the media that morning.

"Listen," Adam said, "there's something I need to tell you. I didn't mention it last night, but Kate Shaw was the one who was murdered."

The shock was clear on her face. "Oh, dear Lord, Adam. What in the world is going on?"

"We don't know for sure yet, but there are similarities between this murder, Ann's, and the woman who was found under the bridge. The news will be all over it today. I've got to be at the station this morning, and I don't want Piper alone when she hears about it. She's still sleeping, and I probably won't be here when she gets up. I know it's asking a lot, but just try to reassure her that everything's going to be okay."

Adam could see indignation gathering on Tracy's face. "Everything is not going to be okay, Adam. I know your friends at the department have been working hard on Ann's case. But it's been over a year, and they've come up with nothing. Now it's getting worse. How am I supposed to tell Piper everything's going to be all right? She's smart enough to know better. Her mother's been killed, and now the therapist who helped her deal with *that* is dead."

"I know," Adam said. "You're right. Please just do what you can. I need to go now. I'll call you."

The weather had turned overnight. As he drove across the James Island Connector, a line of menacing black clouds slid off the ocean, dragging sheets of rain across Charleston Bay and machine-gunning the roof of the Charger. The storm felt like a pretext to the chaos that would engulf the city once Shaw's murder hit the public. He parked the car and was soaked by the time he made it to the door of the station.

Marcus wasn't in yet, and Adam headed up to the Kennels. Detective Charles was at her desk. "Where's Manson?"

"Catching a nap in the Bunkhouse. He spent the night."

"How about Agent Wells?"

"She's in the small conference room. Sergeant told me she's been up all night with those patient files." Claire checked her watch. "She wants to see us before we interrogate Knight and Scott. You go ahead, and I'll get Matt."

Files covered the small conference table in Wells' makeshift office, and the white board on the far wall was filled with a chart she'd apparently drawn. When Stone entered, she simply nodded and returned to the file she was studying, dark semicircles under her eyes.

"Detectives Charles and Manson will be here shortly," Adam said.

That brought a faint smile to her face. "Charles Manson? I like that." She began clearing space at the table, and a moment later, Claire and Matt entered, nodded, and took seats.

Wells continued organizing, paying little attention to them until she finally climbed out of her head and said, "I wanted to go over a few items before Mr. Knight and Mr. Scott are brought in." Wells gestured to the chart on the wall. "I've summarized the identifiers for the four murders in this chart. You can see the victims listed across the top and the identifiers—location, cause of death, weapon used, toxicology, etc.—are listed vertically. What we want to do is determine which identifiers are consistent across all four murders. This will help us understand the similarities and, hopefully, the motive. I apologize for my lack of neatness, but I will prepare a formal chart that can be distributed to all personnel involved with this. It's my understanding that the suspects are being picked up now. Detective Manson, you obtained the warrants. What do they cover?"

"Sure. We have warrants to search their apartments, and we've gotten the green light to have Omni T1200 GPS tracking devices placed on their vehicles. Knight drives a 2004 Chevy Cavalier and Scott a 2007 Dodge Neon. These trackers can be programed to report the vehicle's position at different times when it's stationary as well as follow it when it begins to move. Claire and I will have the app on our phones, plus it will also be installed on the desk sergeant's computer. That way their location and movements can be monitored 24/7. The warrants cover any item that could be related to the Stone, Hanson, Richardson, or Shaw killings. We'll wait until they've left their apartments before the warrants are exercised. We don't want Knight or Scott to know their apartments have been searched or that GPS devices have been secured to their vehicles."

Wells pointed to the identifier labeled *Tox Screen*. "There were traces of propofol in two out of the first three victims. There's a good chance the autopsy will find traces of it in Shaw. The public knows about the candle. Now it's even more critical the detail regarding the propofol remain confidential."

Stone and Charles Manson nodded their agreement.

"Regarding these suspects, we have to remember that their moderate-to-severe mental illness does not mean they aren't intelligent, nor does it preclude their ability to meticulously plan and carry out murders such as these. Dr. Shaw was the second therapist murdered which increases the probability one of her patients committed the murder. We know Knight is still being treated by Dr. Shaw, but Tyler Scott is no longer under the care of a therapist. To be honest, I'm not sure which situation is more likely to point toward guilt. We need to follow the evidence but still keep an open mind."

Agent Wells looked at her watch. "All right, Chief Taylor's meeting starts in twenty minutes. We'll begin the interviews with Knight and Scott afterward."

Wells started putting her files away, and Charles Manson stood to leave when Adam spoke up. "Hold on. I've got something else."

"Go ahead, detective."

"This may be nothing," Adam said, and pointed to the chart on the whiteboard, "but the identifier charts reminded me of another link. We know both my wife and Kate Shaw used the same accountant—a man named Bill Bennett. We also used him for our personal taxes. I never knew him that well, but he seemed like a decent guy. After Ann's funeral, I used him to handle probate and file the necessary papers for her will and business. Something odd happened one day when I was leaving his office. He said he'd 'light a candle for Ann.' He's super religious, and maybe this is just a coincidence. But he grew up in Atlanta, and that's where Hanson was killed. Plus, he was Ann's only appointment the day she was killed. At first, we all figured he was one of the prime suspects, but nothing was ever found to link him to her murder. Also, I knew Claire and Matt came up with nothing suspicious when they interviewed him. I guess I was too focused on the Bloods and Knight and Scott."

Wells put both hands on the table and leaned forward. "I said we need to keep our minds open. Adam, take another look at the chart again. Anything else about him come to mind?"

Stone stared at the chart for a moment and then said, "Holy shit! I can't believe I missed it."

"Missed what?" Claire asked, her interest now piqued.

"The Richardson murder! Bennett's office is on Coleman Boulevard. Sally Richardson lived on Coleman!"

The possibility Bennett might be involved was gathering steam when Manson jumped in. "And Coleman Boulevard runs right into the Ravenel Bridge. That's right where the groundskeeper found her body!"

"God damn it!" Adam said through clenched teeth. "I'm sorry. Bennett seemed like one of those people you just, I don't know, you just overlook—one of those people you walk past every day on the street and don't even notice."

"You wouldn't be the first to be fooled by appearances," Well said. "A good percentage of serial killers seem to be normal, average people. Most who knew Ted Bundy described him as a charming man. Jeffrey Dahmer was considered thoughtful and caring, and Phillip Markoff, the infamous Craigslist Killer, was a member of the National Honor Society and served on his school's student council."

"Now the question is how do we handle Bennett," Manson said.

"I don't think that'll be too difficult," Wells said. "Detective Stone, you've known him for a fair amount of time. I suggest you approach him and say your department is trying to talk to everyone who knew Dr. Shaw. Present it as, 'we need your help.' We don't want to spook him. Make it sound like the department still knows almost nothing about the killing. Maybe he'll let something slip."

Adam was still shaking his head. "He just seemed like the kind of upstanding churchgoer that you aren't supposed to worry about. How can someone like that be a serial killer?"

"I think you'd be surprised," Wells said with a weary smile. "Bundy was a practicing Mormon while he was raping and murdering what could've been up to 100 women."

Knight and Scott were brought in and questioned for about an hour each with nothing substantially new being learned. As soon as their apartments had been searched and the tracking devices secured to their vehicles, Knight and Scott were released. Nothing was found in Scott's apartment other than the Bible, rosary, and images of Jesus that Adam had previously discovered. And nothing of substance was found in Knight's. The search was a bust with the exception of the GPS devices. Nothing at all was uncovered that could connect either suspect to any of the murders.

# CHAPTER TWENTY-THREE
### Monday, April 8

MERCHANT'S COMMENT ABOUT the *shit hitting the fan* when word got out on the Shaw murder was a magnificent understatement. The main conference room at Lockwood was overflowing with reporters and TV cameras. All the local TV and print news outlets were there plus stringers representing the national media. Bad news travels fast, and within an hour, news of "Charleston's Candle Killings" was splashed across the national news—in addition to going viral online.

As suggested by Agent Wells, Adam arranged to meet Bennett the following morning at his Mt. Pleasant office.

"Bill, I'm really sorry to bother you with this, but with the recent murders my chief told me to go back and talk to everyone who'd been in any way associated with Ann when she was killed. I remember you had that meeting scheduled with her the day she disappeared. I know she was gone when you got to her office, but can you remember anything else about that day that might help us? Did you see or talk to anyone while you were waiting at her office?"

Bennett's body language showed he wasn't pleased about being questioned again, but said, "I can understand that. But the answer is still no. I think I told you that when Ann's door was locked and she didn't answer my phone call, I tried Kate's office. She didn't answer, either."

"Right. Ann had that little lime-green Fiat. Can you remember if it was in the lot when you got there?"

"No. I mean, no I can't remember."

"How about any other cars?" Adam pushed.

"No. I wish I could help, but that was more than a year ago."

"I know, but we haven't come up with anything that would help solve her murder. Take your time. Can you think of anything else from that day?"

Bennett again said he remembered nothing.

Adam didn't let up. "I think I remember you saying you went home right after you stopped at Ann's office that day. Isn't that right?"

"I might have. Why do you ask?"

"I don't know, Bill. You're an accountant. Just seems a little strange that you'd go home in the middle of the afternoon during tax season."

"I can't remember. If I did, I probably had something to take care of at home that day. I work for myself you know."

"I know. Just seemed unusual you never checked in with your office until the following day."

It was clear Bennett was getting more and more uncomfortable with Adam's questions. "Look it, Adam. I wish I could help you, but I've told you everything I remember. And I'm starting to get the impression you think I had something to do with Ann's death."

Adam waited a few seconds before responding, "No, not at all. We're just trying to solve a murder."

"Well, I don't have anything else to say about that. Adam, I've spent the last year praying for Ann. And I'll continue to do that. I just hope He answers my prayers. Now, I do need to get back to work."

"I understand, Bill. We appreciate your prayers." Adam stood and they shook hands. "And I'm sure you'll let us know if any of those prayers are answered."

Adam left Bennett's office knowing he'd shaken the man up. Charles Manson increased their focus on Bennett. He was surveilled for several weeks, but nothing new was uncovered. Eventually, warrants were issued for his office and home. Again, no incriminating evidence was found, adding to an already frustrating investigation.

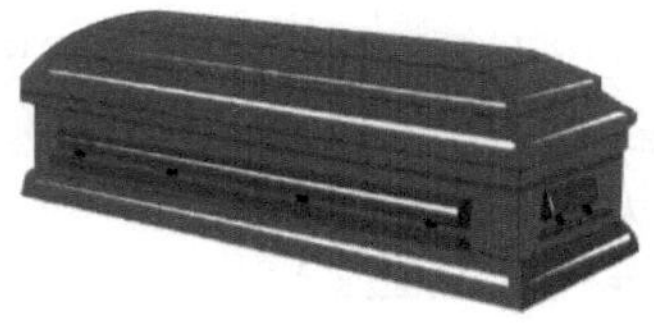

# CHAPTER TWENTY-FOUR

Sunday, April 7

THE KILLINGS REMAINED the lead story on the national outlets for the next several days and dominated the local and regional news for weeks after that. Despite intensive investigations, the department was once again frustrated with a lack of progress on the latest murder. Tourism plummeted. News Channel 5's Chelsey Wallace began a series of reports on each of the four murders. It was hard on Tracy and Piper with Ann's name constantly dragged through the media. Every day felt like a new episode of Law and Order, Criminal Minds, or NCIS.

~~~~

After months of anxiety, tourism had all but returned to its previous levels, and the city's nightlife was again alive and kicking. It was as if the city were breathing again. Summer was in full swing with the beaches packed, the smell of suntan lotion in the air. The resurgence came despite little progress on the murders. Slowly, detectives moved on to other cases, and officers returned to their normal beats. Agent Wells was called back to Quantico in early May, and while the local FBI remained on the case, it was no longer garnering priority attention from headquarters. Charles Manson continued to work the murders, but they were becoming increasingly discouraged with their inability to move the cases forward. While no one would admit it, they had simply run out of leads. The cases were beginning to feel "cold." Despite this, the warrants authorizing the GPS trackers on Knight and Scott's cars remained active.

Adam and Marcus were now working with the FBI on an investigation of a motorcycle gang called the Warlocks. These bikers were part of a regional auto theft ring that specialized in "car cloning," a newer scam where VIN numbers on stolen cars are swapped out for legally registered ones. The stolen vehicle is then sold to an unsuspecting buyer, who isn't compensated when the vehicle is found and confiscated and may even be prosecuted for driving a stolen vehicle.

The investigation was gaining momentum, and Adam was spending more and more time on the case. Both he and Marcus immersed themselves in the world of these bikers. They
~~~~

became familiar with some of the individuals in the gang; men with names like Hurricane, Showtime, Magoo, Chicken, and The Little Professor. These bikers even had names for their bikes like Flying Banana, The Vibrator, Beasty, and Hulk. However, there was nothing humorous about what Adam and Marcus were faced with. These bikers were not your "Weekend Warriors." They were hardened criminals living in a violent and unforgiving world. The man who joined them in the investigation was an FBI agent by the name of Ed Walker. Walker had previously worked undercover in several California biker gangs and was familiar with all the language and customs of these gangs. He was eventually able to infiltrate the Warlocks and get "Patched"—which meant he had passed the initiation and was accepted into the gang.

What little free time Adam did have he spent on the street looking for whatever clues he could find on Ann's murder case. He also kept files from all four killings locked in a closet in his office. He'd unlock the door, usually late at night, and pore over the information looking for anything he might have missed that would move the investigation forward. Knight and Scott remained the prime suspects, but Bennett was now in the mix, too. Any detective worth his salt will tell you there's more to solving a case than physical evidence alone. Instinct plays a huge part—sometimes you just need to follow your gut and temper the rational with the intuitive. Despite the over-whelming evidence pointing to Knight and Scott, Adam's gut wouldn't let him pass on Bennett. That Bennett's office was near the scene of Sally Richardson's murder seemed to be the

only hard evidence pointing at him. But Adam had also discovered that Bennett was in Atlanta attending his twentieth high
school union the same weekend Camila Hanson's body was
discovered. Plus, Hanson worked at Emory University
Hospital, and Bennett had graduated from Emory University
which was affiliated with the hospital.

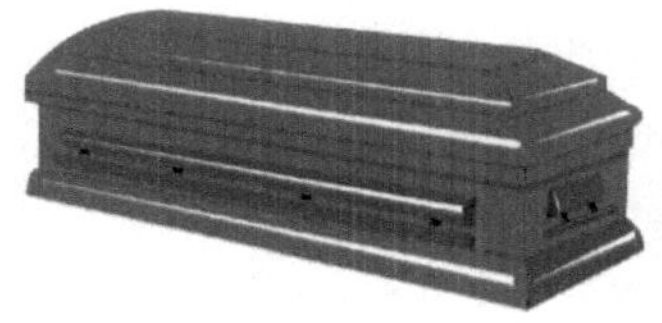

# CHAPTER TWENTY-FIVE
### Friday, August 2

IT HAD BEEN almost four months since Kate Shaw's murder. A wet blanket covered the city as the summer's heat and drenching humidity had the Lowcountry securely in its grip. It was late Friday afternoon, and Adam and Marcus were wrapping up their day when Marcus asked, "Hey, partner, what's up with you this weekend?"

"Lisa's working at the hospital tonight until 11:00, and I promised Piper I'd take her and Chloe to the RiverDogs' game tonight at the Joe. I haven't been around for her lately." Adam smiled and continued, "Both Piper and Chloe are sleeping over at one of their friend's house Saturday, so I've got Lisa all to myself tomorrow night. We're having dinner downtown. Why don't you and Makayla join us?"

"Love to, brother, but I've got 'Station Rotation' this weekend." Station Rotation was a program where each detective was required to spend one weekend every five weeks covering the 6:00 p.m. to 6:00 a.m. shift at the Lockwood station.

"Sorry," Adam said, "I forgot. That sucks."

"It does, but you two deserve some quality time together."

"You got that right. It doesn't happen often, and we're going to take advantage of it. After dinner, I get to spend the whole night with Lisa at my place."

Marcus laughed, "That's cool. Don't forget to get some sleep Saturday night!"

"Sleep?" Adam said, "Hadn't even thought about that!"

~~~~

Joe Riley Stadium, or "The Joe" as it is warmly referred to, is home to the Yankee's Class A minor league affiliate, the Charleston RiverDogs. It's located on the banks of the Ashley River and has always been one of Adam's favorite places. Catching a game at The Joe with Piper is a special treat for both of them, and Friday night was no exception. The evening was topped off with a RiverDog's victory and a fireworks display. Since Lisa was working late, Chloe spent the night with Piper at the apartment. Like typical teenagers, they stayed up most of the night, and Adam let them sleep in when he left the following morning for his regular Saturday basketball games.
~~~~

It was one of the few Saturdays that Piper didn't have a soccer game, and Adam took Max and the girls to the beach that afternoon before dropping the two of them off at Sophia's house for their sleepover.

Adam had 6:00 reservations at the Charleston Grill, an up-scale restaurant on King Street, and was looking forward to a quiet evening with Lisa. The food and drinks were outstanding, and on the way home they decided to stop at the small park on the Stono River where they'd had their first date. It was a nice evening, and they spent an hour or so reminiscing about their time together. After a while, it cooled off, and the breeze picked up. Adam slid his hand around the back of her neck, and they kissed—a kiss that was warm and filled with promise. A moment later, Adam whispered, "Come on, let's go home."

Adam and Lisa made love that night. It was far from the first time they'd been intimate, but this felt somehow different—passionate, but in a softer, deeper way. It was after 1:00 a.m. when they finally fell asleep wrapped in each other's arms.

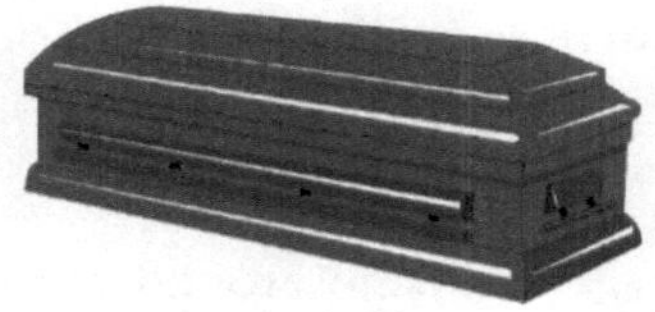

# CHAPTER TWENTY-SIX
Sunday, August 4

HE HAD WATCHED *her small house for several weeks and knew she would return from her waitress job around 1:30 in the morning. He left his car about a mile away, on a cul-de-sac with only three older houses.*

*Her house was a small two-bedroom with a detached garage. Like always, the side door to the garage was unlocked. He'd been waiting inside for an hour. It was dark and humid, and even though he was sweating profusely, the anticipation eased his discomfort. He felt the call of the pack of Newports in his shirt pocket but knew he'd have to wait. He crouched behind an old mattress and box spring propped against the left wall. Right on time, the rusted pulley engaged, and the garage door began to open. She pulled in, cut the headlights, and killed the engine.*

*Erin Brown hadn't even turned around when something hit the back of her neck and her world turned black. He gave her the drug and lifted her into the passenger seat of her car. He drove to the cul-de-sac and transferred her to the trunk of his 2004 Chevy Cavalier.*

~~~~

Lit by the glow of six-foot by three-foot LCD screens, four dispatchers listened for a special tone alerting them to a 911 call. Each dispatcher monitored eight screens linked to the department's central databases and mapping systems. Several flat screens showed the weather, local and national news, and flash images captured from the 37 surveillance cameras around the Lockwood headquarters. With computer banks in every corner, the high-tech call center looked like the set of a Hollywood movie.

The 911 call came into the Lockwood Communication Center at 1:36 a.m.

**Operator:** *911. Is this an emergency?*

**Caller:** *Yeah. I was walking my dog, and I think I saw this guy put someone in the back of his car. I mean in the trunk.*

**Operator:** *Did you get the license number of the vehicle?*

**Caller:** *No, sorry.*

**Operator:** *Can you describe the vehicle?*
~~~~

**Caller:** *Yeah, it was a compact. An old Chevy Cavalier, I'm pretty sure. I think it was blue, but it was dark, you know.*

**Operator:** *Do not attempt to approach the vehicle. I'm dispatching officers to your location. Stay on the line. What is your name?*

**Caller:** *John. John Norman. But he's gone. The guy just drove right past me a minute ago.*

~~~~

Marcus was at his desk relaxing and monitoring 911 dispatch calls when he heard the Code 207 come in. He paid little attention until the vehicle was described as an "old Chevy Cavalier." He knew Charles Knight drove a Cavalier.

Marcus jogged to the desk sergeant and told him to bring up the tracker apps monitoring Knight and Scott. Scott's vehicle was stationary outside his apartment. But Knight's was moving south on I-526. He advised the dispatcher, and she relayed the information to the responding officers.

Adam was asleep when his phone danced across his nightstand and fell to the floor. "Shit," he grumbled, still half asleep. He retrieved it and whispered, "Yeah?"

"It's Marcus. Lockwood just got a 911 abduction call. We think it's Knight, and he's got someone in his trunk. He's heading south on 526."

Now Stone was wide awake. "Let me think. Is a BOLO out on the car?"
~~~~

"Yeah, it's out, and uniforms are rolling."

"All right, Marcus, stay on the line. I'm leaving now."

Adam was dressed in seconds and slid his Glock into his pocket. A minute later, he was in his Charger heading toward the Johns Island Connector. A thick fog hung low blanketing the city.

"Marcus, what's his 20?"

"He just got on 17 heading west."

"Shit," Adam said. He slammed on the brakes, spun the car around, and hit the accelerator. He turned right and headed west on River Road, paralleling 17.

"Hang on," Marcus said. "Okay, he just turned south onto Main. He's crossing the Limehouse Bridge. You should only be a few miles behind him."

Adam couldn't see more than fifty feet in front of him, but he pressed on down River Road with the kind of speed and guesswork that puts cars in ditches.

"I just hit Main. Where is he?"

"Looks like he's probably a mile or two ahead of you. He just passed Maybank. He's on Bohicket now."

"I'll be there in a minute."

A few minutes later, Marcus said, "Okay, he's probably less than a mile ahead. Hold on. He just turned right onto Old Cabin Road, and it looks like he's stopping."

"I know where he is," Adam said. "There's an abandoned black church out there. Cemetery right behind it."

"Adam, backup should be there in the next few minutes. You need to hold fast."

"Tell them to hurry." Adam tossed his cell on the passenger's seat and slowed as he approached the turnoff to Old Cabin Road. He cut his headlights and pulled to the side of the road a hundred feet or so before the church. His Glock was in ready position when he slid out.

The old stone church was a dingy gray, surrounded with tall grass and weeds from years of neglect. Three giant oaks loomed over it—their limbs covered with tentacles of Spanish moss. The combination of fog and moonlight made the gray strands of moss look like Halloween decorations. A few dozen weathered headstones, most askew at different angles, stood like long forgotten remnants from another time. Not far behind the cemetery, Adam could just make out the still waters of Bohicket Creek.

He crouched low and was approaching the front of the church when he heard a car door open.

Glancing around the corner of the building, he saw the Chevy parked in a weed-covered dirt lot in front of a small cemetery. Charles Knight had just opened the trunk of the Cavalier when the distant wail of police sirens cut through the night. He swung his head around toward the sound just as Stone stepped from behind the church and shouted, "Police! Don't move! Hands above your head!"

Knight froze, obviously surprised to hear the sirens and see Stone. He then slowly turned to face him. The sirens grew louder, and the oscillating blue and red lights flashed through the trees, creating a macabre carnival of color.

Stone took a few steps forward. "Move away from the car!" Knight moved to his right, about ten feet. "Now, get on the ground—hands in front of you!"

Knight didn't move.

"I said get on the fucking ground!"

"No, Detective Stone. I don't think I'll do that. I'm unarmed, you know." He held his arms out to his sides and began to back up. "I'm going to turn around. You wouldn't shoot an unarmed man in the back—now would you, detective?" He slowly turned, and in a quicksilver move, veered to his right behind the Chevy and took off toward the cemetery. Stone started after him as three squad cars pulled onto Old Cabin Road and skidded to a stop, their headlights cutting through the fog and flooding the church and cemetery.

Adam was closing on him when Knight tripped over a gravestone and tumbled to the ground. Adam was on him a second later, Glock pointed at the center of his back. Knight was on all fours and yelling. "All right. All right! You got me. I give up! Don't shoot!"

"Hands over your head, asshole!"

Knight raised his left hand and started to stand. At that instant, Adam knew he'd made a serious mistake. Knight pivoted—bringing his right hand up and around in a wide backhanded arc—the knife slicing deep into Stone's right forearm. The Glock flew out of his hand. Knight then brought the blade back across Stone's shoulder.

Knight took off toward the creek, officers moving quickly behind. "Police! Police! Stop or we'll shoot!"

An officer pointed his weapon at Adam, who screamed, "I'm Detective Stone! CPD!"

By now, Knight was in the water, the officers fanned out in a semicircle at the edge of the bank—their guns extended. "Drop your weapon! Drop your weapon!"

Now waist deep, Knight stopped and turned around. Still gripping his knife, he raised both hands above his head. By this time, Adam was at the water's edge. Blood ran down his right arm and pooled on the ground next to him. He raised his left hand and pointed his gun at Knight. "You son of a bitch. You murdered my wife."

Knight's eyes were fixated on Stone. "No, detective. I freed her soul from the Devil. Satan was within her tempting God's children with the lust of the flesh. I am an instrument of my Lord. God told me to end her life, so she might be cleansed and free of sin. I cleansed them all, Stone! I freed them all from their sins, so they might enter the gates of heaven and have eternal life!"

The officers continued shouting, demanding he drop the knife.

Knight raised his head to the night sky and boomed, "Yea, though I walk through the valley of the shadow of death, I will fear no evil, for thou art with me; thy rod and thy staff they comfort me. Thou preparest a table before me in the presence of my enemies. Thou anoint my head with oil; my cup runneth over. Surely goodness and mercy shall follow me all the days of my life. And I will dwell in the house of the Lord forever!"

When he finished, he looked directly at Stone, brought the knife to his neck and in a staccato voice screamed, "I am the word of God!" He then plunged the knife into the side of his neck and dragged it deep across his throat.

Knight fell to his knees, water now reaching the top of his chest. Blood pulsed from the gash in his neck and his dark eyes remained open as he slowly slid beneath the surface and disappeared.

Their weapons extended in the two-handed shooting position, the officers cautiously moved forward, stopping about ten feet from where the body had disappeared. They held their position until Knight's body slowly rose to the surface—face down, lit by the moonlight.

One of the officers, gun still pointed at the body, called to his partner. "Frank, give me a hand here."

The officer moved forward. "I got him," he said and reached down to grab the body. Suddenly, he stopped. "What the hell?" The body had twitched, and Frank backed up just as Knight exploded from the water, knife raised high. At that instant, Stone and all six officers opened fire, emptying their Glocks in a hail of bullets riddling Knight and throwing his body backwards. The gunfire continued even after his body vanished beneath the dark waters of Bohicket Creek.

As if on cue, the shooting stopped. Everyone remained frozen as a ghostly quiet fell upon the night—broken only by the shrill cries of seagulls escaping the cacophony of gunfire.

Stone dropped his gun and fell to his knees.

Two more squad cars and an EMS van arrived. Two paramedics rushed to Adam, kneeling by the water's edge and bleeding profusely.

"Don't worry about me!" He shouted and pointed to the Cavalier. "There's a woman in the trunk! She's unconscious. Probably drugged."

One of the EMT's left to attend to Erin Brown. She was still alive, but her breathing was labored, pupils dilated, and she was sweating profusely. He immediately applied a respirator to maintain air flow and quickly moved her to the EMS van where an IV was administered. Her blood pressure slowly improved, and she began to stabilize.

A tourniquet was applied to Adam's arm, and he joined Erin Brown in the EMS van. Knight's body was dragged to the shore, and an officer began to cordon off the area. Headquarters was radioed requesting the coroner and a forensics team.

As the EMS van left for the hospital, Adam asked a technician to call Marcus, who answered immediately.

"Adam, are you all right?"

"Cut up a little, but yeah, I'm fine."

"What the hell happened?"

"It was Knight. The son of a bitch killed Ann! He killed all of them! But we got him. He's dead. We got the girl, and she's gonna be okay. They're taking us to the trauma center. Call Tracy and let them know I'm all right. Lisa's at my place. Let her know, too. I'll see you at MUSC. I'll tell you more there."

"You got it, brother."

The grounds around the old church was alive with activity, as the van left for MUSC—lights flashing and siren cutting through the still night air. By the time they got to the MUSC Trauma Center, the paramedics had stabilized Erin Brown and addressed Adam's wounds. They were wheeled through the double doors and ushered into separate curtained treatment rooms.

A few minutes later, a young resident entered, removed Adam's dressings, and inspected the knife wounds. "Not as bad as it could've been, detective. The wound in your forearm made it all the way to your radius bone. That's why you had considerable blood loss. The cut on your shoulder is fairly superficial. We'll get you numbed up and give you something for pain. The nurse will get you another IV. You're going to need about two units of blood. I want you to relax. You're going to be fine. I'll be right back, and we'll get you all sewed up."

Adam was still jacked with adrenaline—relaxing was pretty much out of the question. The forearm required thirty internal and external sutures, and the shoulder wound needed ten. By the time he was stitched up and moved to another room, the sedative and pain medication had him relaxed and sleepy.

Sometime later, he was resting quietly when he heard the door open. He opened his eyes to see Marcus and Lisa standing in front of him.

Marcus pointed to his bandaged right arm and smiled. "Ouch, partner. That must hurt like the devil. How are you feeling?"

Adam shut his eyes. "I feel fine, but can we please leave the Devil out of this?"

Lisa took his left hand and whispered, "I woke up, and you were gone. I was worried sick."

Adam, still groggy from the drugs, said, "You look beautiful. You want to go out sometime?"

Marcus told him to get some rest, and they'd see him in a while. The doctor told Marcus the sedative would begin to wear off in an hour or so, and he could be discharged shortly after that.

"Thanks, doc, we'll wait here and make sure he gets home."

Lisa left, and it was almost 7:00 in the morning by the time Marcus drove Adam back to his apartment. The sedative had pretty much worn off and after taking two pain pills the doctor prescribed, Adam was mellowed out and resting comfortably on the living room sofa.

Marcus asked him if he felt up to telling him what happened at the church. Adam took about five minutes highlighting the events leading up to when Knight was shot. "Christ, you should have seen it. It looked like Sonny Corleone at the tollbooth in the Godfather! Knight admitted he'd killed Ann and the others before we took him out. He was so proud of himself. He said God told him to do it."

Tracy and Piper arrived shortly after that, and Marcus said, "All right, brother, I'm going to take off. You get yourself some rest, and I'll talk to you later."

"Hey, detective," Adam said. "I learned something last night."

"What's that?"

Adam grinned. "You don't bring a knife to a gunfight!"

Marcus laughed and left leaving Tracy and Piper to take care of him. He dozed off and slept most of the afternoon. When he awoke early that evening, Taylor and Merchant were there to check on him. He again recapped what had happened at the church.

"We've got the preliminary statements from the officers who were out there," Merchant said, "but we need you at the station tomorrow to give your formal statement."

"I'll be there."

"That's a hell of a thing you did, Adam," Taylor said. "The whole department's proud of you."

"I don't know about that, Chief. All I know is that it over. Thank God, it's finally over."

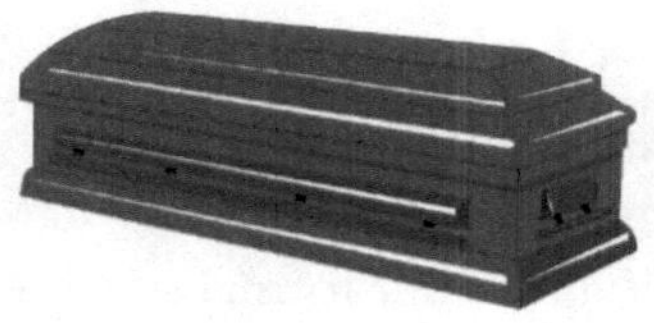

# CHAPTER TWENTY-SEVEN
### Monday, August 5

THE NEXT MORNING Adam, along with Lisa, Piper, Chloe, and Tracy were at the apartment watching television coverage of the press conference. It was standing room only in the main conference room at City Hall. When Mayor Tecklenburg announced that the Charleston serial killer had finally been captured and killed, the room erupted in thunderous applause and cheers.

"I'd like to thank the unwavering dedication of our detectives, police officers, and everyone else involved in bringing this killer to justice," the mayor said. "I want to give a special thanks to Detective Adam Stone. He's at home recovering from injuries he sustained last night. Our city owes him and our entire police department a debt of gratitude for their bravery and dedication to duty."

Later that afternoon, Adam sat in the conference room alongside Merchant, Charles Manson and Marcus. Merchant nodded to Claire, who hit the record button on the tape machine. Merchant stated the date and location and identified himself. "I'm joined by Detectives Adam Stone, Claire Charles, Mathew Manson, and Marcus Williams," he continued. "We're here to record Detective Stone's statement of his involvement in the apprehension and subsequent death of Charles Knight."

When Adam completed his statement, they cut the recording, and Merchant nodded to Claire and Matt. "We know detectives didn't find anything in Knight's apartment when they searched it the first time." Merchant smiled. "Claire, go ahead and tell Adam what the forensic guys discovered this morning in Knight's car."

"First of all, they found a bag full of plastic bottles containing prescriptions of Chlorpromazine and Zofran. The dates on the prescription containers go back well over a year. Why the hell he kept those, we'll never know. Based on the specific dates, some of those periods corresponded with each of the four murders.

"And get this. One of the techs was going through Knight's trunk, and he found this small box taped to the bottom of the spare tire cover. After it was photographed and dusted for prints, one of the forensic technicians opened it. It held plastic baggies containing locks of hair with dates matching the four murders we know of. But there's also five other locks of hair with dates preceding Ann's death. Plus, there were four necklaces with dates attached. All will be tested for DNA. But it looks like Knight could have been responsible for as many as nine other murders. Hopefully, this will lead to solving some outstanding cold cases. I can't imagine how he flew under the radar all these years."

Merchant looked at Adam. "I know none of this will bring back Ann, but at least we got him, and maybe this will give some families the closure they need. We can take solace in that possibility. Adam, you've been through hell this last year and a half. I want you to take some time off and spend it with your family. Take whatever time you need. When you're ready, I need you back."

~~~~

Exactly two weeks after they took out Knight, Adam dropped off Piper for the start of her freshman year at Charleston Collegiate. He sat in his car watching her walk away and thinking how much she'd grown, and about how much their lives had changed over the last year and a half. He'd lost Ann—his first true love. It was a nightmare—one he wasn't sure he'd ever wake up from. Who knows what the future might hold? He pulled out of the school's parking lot and headed downtown.

On the way, he stopped at The Cup for two coffees and two croissants. He walked into the bullpen and took a seat
~~~~

across from Marcus. After putting a coffee and croissant on Marcus' desk, he said, "All right, brother, I'm back. Are you ready to catch some bad guys?"

Marcus picked up the roll and coffee and shook his head. "Do you mind if I finish these first, brother?"

"All right but hurry up. I'm ready to be a cop again."

~~~~
~~~~

Coming in 2021 …

# PRIME SUSPECTS

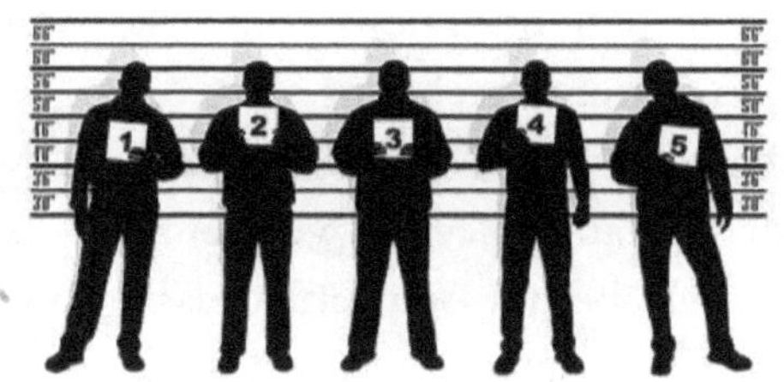

# CHAPTER 1

MOST PEOPLE VIEWED Joe Wallace as a person only a mother could love. Truth be told, Joe's mother wasn't all that fond of him either. He did, however, possess some impressive credentials: law degree from Harvard, clerked for a prominent appellate judge, and was poised to become a partner in the prestigious Charleston law firm of Jones, Sanders, and Cole. His success in the courtroom had garnered him a reputation as one of Charleston's premier defense attorneys.

More important than his legal prowess was the fact that he was married to Elizabeth Buckley, the daughter of Edward Buckley, the patriarch of one of the richest and most influential families in Charleston. Even in these modern times, there are only two ways to become accepted into traditional Charleston society: birthright or marriage. After twenty years of marriage to Elizabeth, Wallace was not shy about taking advantage of the perks his place in the Buckley family afforded him. He also had developed a rather dubious reputation as a heavy drinker, gambler, and frequent user of various controlled substances—not to mention his notoriety for chasing skirt.

After twenty years of marriage to Elizabeth, Wallace knew where most of the family secrets were buried—secrets that, if made public, would be not only embarrassing but also lead to some serious legal consequences for the family. Elizabeth was not blind to her husband's exploits, but Joe had made it crystal clear that he would drag her precious family through the mud should she ever tried to divorce him. His threat had nothing to do with his feelings toward his wife and everything to do with the financial and personal benefits he enjoyed as part of the Buckley family.

The Honorable Stephen A. Jackson of the Charleston County Circuit Court had just completed jury instructions in the murder trial of Demarco Moore. Moore was a member of Charleston's East Side Posse gang and was on trial for the execution-style murder of Alejandro Ruiz, a member of their rival gang, the Bloods. The two gangs had for some time been battling over control of the drug trade in the Charleston area.

This was not the first time Wallace represented a member of the Posse. Their criminal activities and propensity for violence had made them one of Wallace's more lucrative clients. Not wanting to tarnish their pristine reputation, the partners at the firm funneled all proceeds from legal work done on behalf of the Posse through a wholly owned subsidiary.

Despite the overwhelming evidence clearly identifying Demarco as the killer, Joe's arguments were so convincing that a guilty verdict seemed extremely unlikely.

Both Judge Jackson and the jury had left the courtroom when Wallace's opposing attorney, Thomas Smith, approached him and extended his hand. "You put on quite a show today, Joe, but we both know your boy Demarco's guilty as sin."

Wallace ignored the expected handshake and replied, "I don't give a shit whether he's guilty or innocent. He's going to walk, and we both know it."

Smith shook his head. "Christ, Wallace, you're such a prick."

Joe just smiled and said, "I think I hear an ambulance, Tommy. Why don't you go chase it?"

Wallace finished gathering up his files, left the courtroom, and made the five-minute walk up Queen to Magnolias for a quick lunch. He ordered a Glenlivet single malt scotch and was scanning his messages when he saw one from his bookie, Derrick D. When he opened the message, "$25,000" was all it said. The message was crystal clear. Joe preferred gambling on sports, especially when he'd been drinking, and had rung up a $25,000 debt. He normally wouldn't give it a second thought to this because Elizabeth always covered his debts. However, her asshole father had just frozen her accounts. It wasn't the first time Edward Buckley had done that, but Joe knew that Elizabeth would eventually persuade him to change his mind. The problem was that Derrick D. worked for Nick Santoro. Santoro was connected to the Chicago mob, and they weren't exactly the most patient people.

Wallace knew he'd have to deal with Santoro and his gambling debt, but for now he'd settle for the Glenlivet and his usual prime rib sandwich. He finished his meal and returned to his King Street law office, where he relaxed waiting for the call from Judge Jackson's clerk advising him that the Demarco verdict was in. Another "not guilty" verdict would virtually guarantee what he considered to be his long-overdue partnership at the firm. Joe got the call at 4:00 p.m. and left for the courthouse. He was surprised the call had come in so quickly.

The courtroom was almost full—a good portion being members of both the East Side Posse and the Bloods. There was also a smattering of local news reporters, prosecuting attorneys, and a few of Joe's colleagues from the law firm. The tension in the courtroom was not as pronounced as you might expect in a murder case. In the eyes of many who watched the case unfold, a "not guilty" verdict seemed a foregone conclusion. Judge Jackson entered and took his seat at the bench. He instructed the bailiff to bring in the jury. Joe studied the jurors' faces looking for tells, but they all seemed somber as they filed in and took their seats in the jury box.

Once they were seated, Judge Jackson began with the perfunctory thank-yous to the jury for their patience and attention during the trial. He then asked the foreperson to stand. "I understand you have reached a decision."

"Yes, Your Honor, we have."

The bailiff retrieved the verdict sheet from the foreperson and presented it to the judge. Jackson glanced at the sheet and gave it back to the bailiff, who returned it to the foreperson. The judge said, "Will the defendant please stand?" Demarco Moore and Joe stood. The judge nodded toward the foreperson and continued, "You may read the verdict."

"In the first count, murder in the first degree, the jury finds the defendant, Demarco Moore, guilty as charged." The foreperson went on to confirm guilty verdicts for the remaining three counts.

The judge, his gaze still focused on the jury, said, "So say you all?"

The entire jury responded, "Yes, Your Honor."

"The court thanks you for your service. You are now free to go. Bailiff, you may remove the defendant." The judge banged his gavel once. "Court is adjourned."

Joe Wallace couldn't believe his ears. There must be some kind of mistake. Demarco Moore turned to him and said, "What the fuck?"

There was a commotion in the back of the courtroom, and Joe looked behind him. Byron "Spider" Brown was staring back at him—his eyes burning with menace. Brown was the shot caller for the East Side Posse. He shook his head once and left the courtroom, followed by four of his underlings.

The bailiff and two officers removed Moore from the courtroom. Wallace slumped back into his chair, still trying to process what had just happened. He was positive he had this one nailed.

Prosecuting attorney Thomas Smith walked over to Wallace. "Hey, Joe. Do you hear that?"

Wallace, still numb from the verdict, said, "Hear what?"

"Sounds like an ambulance. Why don't you go chase it?"

~~~

The courtroom was almost empty, and Joe was still seated at the defense table. *What the hell just happened?* He'd had an impressive string of "not guilty" verdicts but knew that would mean nothing to Spider Brown. Brown had already shelled out a $75,000 retainer fee, but that didn't cover the cost of the trial. Plus, a loss like this wouldn't sit well with the partners at Jones, Sanders, and Cole and his shot at becoming a partner. But right now, that was the least of his worries. He owed Nick Santoro twenty-five big ones, and he didn't have the money.
~~~

# CHAPTER 2

DETECTIVES ADAM STONE and Marcus Williams sat quietly in the back of the courtroom watching the spectators file out.

Marcus turned to Adam. "Well, brother, it looks like our friend Demarco is on his way up shit's creek without a paddle."

Adam smiled. "Can't say that breaks my heart."

Both Stone and Wallace had put in almost twenty years as members of the Charleston Police Department, the last six as partners working in Captain Ed Merchant's elite Special Operations Division. The two detectives could not have looked more different—almost like a *Mutt and Jeff* thing. Marcus was 6'

4" and pushing 250 pounds. His chest and arms were huge. His neck seemed to be missing, his shaved ebony black head merely an extension of his shoulders. Despite his massive size, it was his eyes that drew your attention. Eyes that were clear, cool, and profoundly intelligent.

In contrast, Adam was white, a few inches shy of 6', and a slender but solid 185. Their backgrounds were just as dissimilar. Adam was raised in the upper middle class, predominately white Charleston suburb of Mount Pleasant, and Marcus grew up in the rough-and-tumble Union Heights section of North Charleston. Despite their differences, they consistently led the department in the number of closed cases.

Adam and Marcus headed up a task force that investigated the constantly changing landscape of the illicit drug trade in Charleston. There was never a lack of players involved in the effort to control the distribution of heroin and cocaine in the city. Adam and Marcus had been at the center of a recent major drug bust that had upset the balance of power and set the stage for another battle to control the trade. The first victim in the battle was Alejandro Ruiz. He took a bullet to the back of his head, allegedly fired by the Posse's Demarco Moore.

Approximately six months ago, fentanyl-laced heroin began showing up on the street. The potent concoction led to a rash of serious overdoses and several deaths. It was discovered that the drug was being brought into the States by the Sinaloa Cartel and sold on the street by members of the East Side Posse. This led to the creation of Operation Orion, a coordinated effort between the task force, FBI, and DEA resulting in the recovery of thirty kilos of product, $3 million in cash, and the arrest of Odell Davis, the shot caller for the East Side Posse.

"There's already a shitload of bad blood between the Posse and the Bloods," Adam said, "and the Demarco verdict is bound to kick it up a few notches. Plus, you've got MS-13, the cartel, the Chicago mob, and a few more wannabes that will probably make a play. I wouldn't be surprised if we've got another gang war on our hands."

"Right. Ever since the Posse's Odell Davis was convicted and sent away for drug trafficking, Spider Brown's been looking to make a name for himself. Sometimes I wonder how the hell we're supposed to stay on top of all this shit."

Marcus checked his watch. "Let's take off. I got a text from Merchant. He said one of the Bloods was just picked up on an outstanding warrant. The guy's name is Walter White." Marcus smiled. "Yeah, Walter White—just like *Breaking Bad*. Ed said he's one of their enforcers. They've got him down at Lockwood."

Adam and Marcus arrived at the Lockwood station and asked the desk sergeant where White was being held and the reason for the outstanding warrant.

"Big son of a bitch," the sergeant said. "Shaved head, tattoos—the whole nine yards. Officer pulled him over for running a stop sign and get this: he ran the guy's plates and pulled up an outstanding bench warrant for parking tickets! They got him down the hall in Room One. Have fun, fellas."

"I'll give you the honors," Adam said, leaving for the observation room to view Marcus's interview with White. Interrogation Room One and Room Two were separated by a smaller room from which both could be observed and videotaped through two-way mirrors.

Marcus entered Room One. White was seated at a metal table in the small 10' x 10' interrogation room. The room was stark—bright florescent lights, no window, no clock, no connection whatsoever to the world outside its four dingy gray walls. The sergeant wasn't kidding in the way he described White. He resembled a bowling ball. Looked to be about 5' 10", weighing well over 250. However, it was obvious there was plenty of muscle mixed in with the fat. White stared at Marcus but said nothing.

"Mr. White, I'm Detective Williams." Marcus considered the clipboard he held and said, "Says here you've got $1,386 worth of outstanding parking tickets, and you missed your court date."

"This is bullshit," White said. "Parking tickets? Jesus Christ, I'll pay the fuckers!"

Marcus glanced at his watch. "I'm afraid that's not gonna happen, Walter. It's after 6:00 on Friday, and there's no bail hearings over the weekend. Monday morning's gonna be the earliest we can get you in to see the judge. You're probably going to spend the weekend at the North Charleston Detention Center. I can't promise anything but work with me and I'll see what I can do."

White was suspicious. "What the hell does that mean, and where's my wheels?"

"I'm sure your car's been towed to our Leeds Avenue impound lot. But like I said, answer a few questions and I'll see what I can do."

"What questions?"

"Word is you run with the Bloods. That right, Walter?"

"Yeah, I hang with them. So what?"

"Just wondering, that's all. Where do you work, Walter?"

White smiled. "I do my own thing. I'm one of them entrepreneurs."

"How's that working out for you?"

"Workin' out just fine."

"I take it you know Spider Brown." Brown had moved up to the position of shot caller for the Posse once Odell Davis was convicted and incarcerated.

White said nothing. Marcus repeated, "Walter. You know Spider, right?"

After a moment, White said, "Yeah, I know who he is."

"Word on the street is Spider dropped a Code Red on the Bloods."

"I don't know shit about that. You said you were gonna help me out."

Marcus stood and walked toward the door. "Right, Walter. Just sit tight. I'll be right back."

As soon as Marcus got back in the observation room, Adam said, "So, what now?"

"Let's let our friend, Walter, sit for the weekend. That'll give us time to take a look at his place."

"No way are we getting a warrant," Adam said.

"I know, but that's no reason we can't check it out. Listen, why don't you go in and shake him up. I say we put a tail on him when he's cut loose Monday morning. See what he does—who he sees."

"Works for me," Adam said and left for the interrogation room. He entered Room One and said, "Let's cut the bullshit, White. Who's supplying your smack?"

"What are you talking about?"

"Heroin, Walter. Who's supplying the Bloods?"

"This is bullshit. Where's the other guy. I want to talk to him."

"Have a nice weekend, Walter." Adam left the room.

~~~~

A despondent Joe Wallace left the courthouse and made the five-minute walk to his King Street office. He had no doubt that the Demarco Moore verdict had already hit the street, and the partners at Jones, Sanders, and Cole knew the verdict. He went directly to his office without so much as a nod to his secretary. "Hold my calls, Judy. I don't want to be disturbed." He was about to close the door when she said, "Mr. Jones wants to see you in his office."

"Tell him I'm on a conference call and I'll see him later." Wallace shut the door, tossed his briefcase on his Chesterfield
~~~~

leather couch, headed directly to his Baroque walnut desk, and removed a bottle of Chivas from its bottom drawer. He poured himself a healthy shot and downed it. *What the fuck just happened?*

It had been more than a year since he'd lost a case, and that was only a third-rate embezzlement suit. He'd been untouchable when it came to murder cases. His eyes arced around his palatial office. He'd grown accustomed to its elegant surroundings—Kashan oriental rugs, Paul Calle original paintings, mahogany paneled walls, stone fireplace. No one deserved it more than he did. He was gazing out of his sixth-floor window at Charleston Harbor when he heard his office door open.

Without turning around, he said, "Damn it, Judy. I said I didn't want to be disturbed!"

"How was your conference call, Joe?"

Wallace turned around to see Howard Jones and Matthew Cole standing at his office door.

"Hope we're not interrupting, Joe," Jones said with a rather feigned smile, "but Matt and I would like a few words with you."

"Of course, Howard." He nodded at Cole. "Please have a seat."

"Thanks Joe," Jones replied, "but this won't take long. What happened today?"

"Hell, Joe. We knew Demarco was guilty when we took the case."

"Excuse me, Joe," Matt Cole said, "but I seem to remember you were the one who convinced us to take it on. I think you said it was 'a slam dunk.'"

"That's okay, Matt," Jones interjected. "You know what they say: 'You can't win 'em all.'"

Joe started to relax a bit when Jones continued. "But we sure as hell need to be paid for the ones you lose. Right, Joe?" He turned to Cole. "Matt, how much does Joe's client still owe the firm?"

"Funny you should ask, Howard. I just checked, and Joe's client owes us another $75,000 and change."

The smile left Jones's face. "We expect that to be paid in the next thirty days. That won't be a problem, will it, Joe?"

"Of course not," Wallace said. "I've represented them before, and we've never had a problem."

"That's true," Matt said, "but you've never lost before." Jones and Cole left the room without another word.

Joe remembered the look on Spider Brown's face when the "not guilty" verdict was announced. He wasn't at all sure the Posse would pay up this time. "Judy, get my wife on the phone."

The Chivas was still on his desk. He needed another drink to calm his nerves. But before he could pour one, Judy was at his door. "I'm sorry, Mr. Wallace, but your wife's out of the country. Your maid said she's on a cruise and won't be back until next Wednesday. Do you want me to call Mr. Buckley?"

"No!" Edward Buckley was the last person Joe wanted to know he was in a financial shithole. It was no secret that Elizabeth's father despised him. A darkness fell over Joe that not even the glow of the Chivas could penetrate. "Shut the door and leave me alone."

Judy closed the door and smiled to herself. She'd worked for Joe Wallace for three years and thought he was a horse's ass. She was tired covering for his drinking, gambling, and whoring. It was about time he finally got what he deserved.

Joe knew he was in trouble. He owed Nick Santoro twenty-five grand, and he knew there was a chance Spider wasn't going to make good on the balance of the Posse's legal bill. And his bank had made it clear that there'd be no more loans unless his father-in-law cosigned the note. In the past, Joe had even borrowed from the street, knowing that Elizabeth would cover the debt and weekly vig. But that wouldn't work this time—Santoro controlled the city's loansharking racket. He needed to get out of the office and go somewhere he could think.

Joe spent most of his time after work at the Harbour Club, a private club overlooking downtown's Waterfront Park with a panoramic view of Charleston Bay. However, when he was in the mood for some serious drinking and carousing, he'd head to Salty's on East Montague in North Charleston. It was still light when he pulled his Audi A7 into the parking lot next to Salty's. He entered the bar, pausing a minute and allowing his eyes to adjust to the dim surroundings. It was a Friday, but the place was dead. Two men were nursing beers and watching ESPN at the far end of the bar. The six booths against the wall were empty. Joe slipped off his suit coat, loosened his tie, and took a chair at the bar.

The bartender nodded at him. "What can I get you, Joe?"

"Chivas on the rocks, Tony." He downed the scotch, the whiskey sliding across his tongue—the warm and familiar burn following behind. He returned the glass to the bar and pointed to it. Tony poured another.

As the evening wore on, Joe's confidence increased with each successive drink. He thought to himself, *Spider's gonna pay up. He just needs a little time to cool off. And the firm needs me. I'm a fucking rainmaker! Hell, I bet Howard would even front me the twenty-five grand to pay off Santoro.*

By 9:00 p.m., Joe had a serious buzz on. He was feeling mellow, and his mood had definitely improved. He was watching the Hornets/Celtics game on the TV when the door opened, and a couple entered the bar. The guy was a big dude with a shaved head and arms covered with tatts. It was clear Salty's wasn't the first bar the two had visited that night. The girl was tall and well put together, although it was clear she had a good number of miles on her. She wore skintight leggings and one of those cutoff T-shirts that left little to the imagination. They sat a few seats down from Joe and ordered two beers and two shots of Windsor. Joe stared at her for a while before his attention shifted back to the game. He did, however, continue to check her out. Eventually, he caught her eye, tipped his glass, and winked at her. He was somewhat surprised when she smiled back and blew him a kiss. She turned and said something to the guy she was with. They both laughed.

The game had just finished, with Boston trouncing Charlotte by 20. Joe was pissed. He had dropped $500 on the Hornets, figuring they'd cover the 12-point spread. "Jesus,

Tony, that's four in a row those bums have lost. Remind me to never bet on them again!" His attention swung back to the T-shirt woman. She was now sitting by herself—the tatt guy must have gone to the head.

He called out to the bartender and pointed to the woman. His words were a bit slurred. "Hey, Tony, *gets* that lovely lady a drink. On me."

Tony pulled out a bottle of Bud from the cooler, opened it, and placed it in front of the woman. She gave Joe a seductive smile and mouthed, "Thank you, baby."

Joe stood, grabbed his drink, and made his way down the bar to where the woman was seated. "You, my dear, are a beautiful lady. What's your name?"

"Bella." Her speech was also showing the effects of the several shots and beers she'd consumed over the last few hours. "Thanks for the drink."

"You're very welcome, Bella. I was wondering …" But before he could say another word, Joe noticed her eyes had shifted away from him and toward the rear of the bar. He turned and saw her tattooed boyfriend leaving the restroom.

The smile left T-shirt's face. "You probably ought to go back to your seat, baby."

That was solid advice. However, Joe was full of liquid courage and pointed to Tattoo. "Tony, get that fella another beer. Put it on my tab." Tony took two steps to his right, reached under the bar, and took ahold of the handle of his sawed-off baseball bat.

Joe raised his glass to the tattooed man and said, "Hello there, my friend. Name's Joe Wallace."

The next thing Joe knew, his drink was flying across the room, and Tattoo had ahold of his shirt. "Take a fucking hike, asshole!"

"Take it easy, man!" Joe said. "No harm, no foul. I got the message!"

Tattoo swung Joe around and pushed him back down the bar. "Hey, Tony, tell Mr. Businessman to get the hell out of here before I lose my temper."

Still holding the bat, Tony said, "Joe, you need to leave. Forget about your tab. It's on the house."

"All right! All right!" Joe said. "I'll leave. Just need to get my jacket. This is a fucking dive anyway."

Joe turned, but before he took another step, he grabbed the bottle of Bud he'd bought for Bella, spun around, and smashed it across the side of Tattoo's head. It exploded, sending glass, beer, and blood across the bar onto Bella's face.

Tony was over the bar in a second, bat in hand. He grabbed Joe's coat and threw it to him. "Get out. Get the hell out now!"

Joe caught his coat and was out the door.

Tattoo was sprawled on the floor, blood covering the side of his face. He was dazed but managed to grab the side of the bar and pull himself up. By this time, Tony was in front of him. "Let it go, Bobby! Not worth it. Let the son of a bitch go!"

Tattoo pushed Tony out of the way, burst through the door, and disappeared into the night.

# CHAPTER 3

ADAM STONE LIVED in a Johns Island apartment with his thirteen-year-old daughter, Piper. Almost two years ago, Adam's wife, Ann, was brutally murdered at the hands of what turned out to be a serial killer. Three other women were murdered, and for the next agonizing year, the investigation went nowhere. It was a hellish time for everyone involved. Finally, Adam, along with several police officers, cornered and killed the murderer outside an old abandoned church on Johns Island. Adam's and Piper's lives were now slowly beginning to return to some form of normalcy, even though the heartbreak and pain of Ann's loss would always be with them.

Perhaps one of the reasons Marcus and Adam worked so well together was their love of sports. Marcus was a middle linebacker and a four-year starter at Clemson University. He'd received second-team All-American honors his senior year. Despite his size, Adam had been a decent basketball point guard at Francis Marion University and continued to play in one of the highly competitive downtown Charleston leagues. He also made a point of playing Saturday mornings with a group of guys at a local gym. Now in his forties, he'd lost a few steps but could still hold his own against the younger players. These Saturday morning games were a welcome respite from the pressure and stress of his job.

Piper was not only an exceptional student at Charleston Collegiate but also one of her school's premier soccer players. Adam returned home from basketball, quickly showered, dressed, and drove Piper to her soccer game at her school's Johns Island campus. On the way to the game, Adam picked up Ann's mother, Tracy Kendall. Since Ann's death, Tracy had become even more involved in both Adam's and Piper's lives.

The gamed ended with Charleston Collegiate edging their opponent, 2–1. Adam treated Piper and her friend Chloe White to pizza before heading back to the apartment. Chloe was a classmate of Piper's and the daughter of Lisa White; the woman Adam had been seeing for the past several months. Lisa was a surgical nurse at MUSC. It had been a chance meeting that brought them together. They fell into a comfortable friendship that eventually developed into a somewhat more serious relationship.

Later that afternoon, Adam picked up Marcus at his West Ashley home and left to check out Walter White's place. White's house was located at the end of a cul-de-sac in North Charleston's Midland Park neighborhood. It looked to be a small two-bedroom with a detached garage. There were four other houses on the cul-de-sac, two of which were boarded up. The grounds around the house were overrun with tall grass and weeds, and the house itself was in disrepair. A good-sized pit bull paced back and forth inside a chain link pen.

Adam pulled his Charger over to the side of the road a few hundred feet from the house. "Let's leave the car here. Not sure if White lives alone. You stay here. I'll knock on the door, and if anyone answers, I'll come up with some story—got lost, looking for the Joneses, or something like that."

Marcus laughed. "Yeah, partner. That makes sense. Some lily-white peckerwood comes knockin' on my door in the middle of this neighborhood, I doubt I'd be inclined to invite him in for lemonade. You stay put. I'll do it."

Marcus left the car, approached the house, and knocked. No one answered. He knocked again. After waiting a bit longer, he peered through one of the front windows. The dog started to bark and still no one came to the door. It was clear nobody was in the house, and he gave Adam the all clear. They walked around the house, checking each window as they went, and then moved on to the garage. The side door was locked. After double-checking that no one else was in the area, Adam took out a small leather case, removed a tension tool and pick, and had the padlock opened in a matter of minutes.

The inside of the garage was dark; however, there was enough ambient light to see that it held an SUV. After their eyes adjusted, it was clear that the car was a late-model Chevy Tahoe. The Tahoe's hood was open, and several engine parts had been removed and placed on a nearby workbench.

"Looks like our friend Walter has a hobby," Adam said. "The Tahoe's obviously being chopped."

Hearing the pit bull's persistent barking, Marcus whispered, "Yeah, you're probably right. Come on, we need to get the hell out of here."

Adam held up his hand. "Hang on a second." There was a small metal desk against the far wall. Adam grabbed a rag and opened the center drawer. It contained an assortment of pens and pencils, a stapler, and some other office items—nothing of interest. He was about to return to Marcus when he noticed a small spoon, a Bic lighter, and a few empty small baggies in the corner of the drawer. The bags had been imprinted with three small black skulls. Adam put one of them in his pocket.

They left the garage. Adam closed the door and relocked the padlock. He used his shirt to wipe the lock and door handle.

Once back in the Charger and a half mile down the road from White's house, Marcus said, "Can't say I'm surprised with what we found."

"Right. I looked inside the windshield of the Tahoe, and the VIN plate had been removed. Those were three dime bags I found." Adam removed the baggie and handed it to Marcus. "Looks like Walter has the habit and is supporting it by chopping. I haven't seen those skulls on bags of smack before. The skulls might identify the Bloods' new source for their heroin."

"Yeah, that makes sense," Marcus replied. "Problem is we broke into the place, and there's that little thing called the Fourth Amendment. Fruit of the poisonous tree and all that. We obviously can't use any of this to bust White, but he just might cooperate if he knows what we have on him."

"May be worth a try, but I don't buy it," Adam said. "He knows what will happen to him if he plays 'show and tell' with us. I say we let White know what we found and keep an eye on him. Maybe he'll do something stupid. In the meantime, we can give the skull bag to vice and see if they can chase it down."

~~~~

Adam was on his way back to West Ashley to drop off Marcus when his cell rang. Marcus answered and was quiet for a minute before he said, "We'll be there in twenty minutes."

"What's up, brother?"

"That was Merchant. A floater just washed up on the Ashley close to Higgins Pier. Ed wants us to handle it. Officers are already at the scene."

"Shit, Chloe's spending the night with Piper at the apartment, and I was planning on taking everyone out to dinner tonight."

"Change of plans, my friend."
~~~~

The Higgins Pier was located at the eastern end of the West Ashley Bikeway and was a favorite spot for local fishermen. There were already several bystanders assembled when Adam pulled into the parking area. Officers had the area around the entrance to the pier closed off with crime scene tape.

Adam and Marcus lifted the tape and showed their badges to one of the officers. "What do we have so far?"

"A 911 call came in about forty-five minutes ago. The caller was fishing on the pier and said he saw what looked like a body on the shore about fifty yards downriver." The officer pointed to his left. "He's over there giving his statement to my partner. The coroner and CSI have been notified and should be here shortly. Come on, I'll show you."

It was low tide, and the upper half of the body was on the shore—the rest was partly submerged in pluff mud. They were about twenty-five feet from the body when Marcus grabbed the officer's arm. "Hold on! We don't want to compromise the crime scene." From where they stood, they could see a portion of the victim's head. The face was partially covered with seaweed, and the fish and land crabs had obviously gotten to the eyes. It was definitely a man, and even from that distance, there was no doubt that his throat had been sliced open.

The crime scene techs arrived a few minutes later and began taking pictures of the body and assessing the surrounding area. One of the techs removed the man's wallet. He placed it in an evidence bag and gave it to another tech, who made a notation identifying the manner, time, and place the wallet was removed.

"I don't see any footprints in the mud," Adam said. "The body was probably dumped upriver and carried down with the tide."

Marcus was about to respond when they heard a voice behind him. "Looks like someone decided to take a swim." It was Alice O'Sullivan. O'Sullivan was a Charleston County deputy coroner and had been around for as long as Adam could remember. She was in her mid-fifties, gray-haired, and a bit portly. She wore a pair of baggy work pants, a black sweatshirt, and knee-high rubber boots. "What'd you got for me, detectives?"

Adam smiled. "It's a dead body, Alice."

"No shit. Let's have a look." She slipped on crime scene gloves and, after getting a nod from one of the CSI techs, approached the body. "It's a fresh one. Don't see any evidence of bloating." She attempted to lift one of the man's arms. "Body is still in full rigor. Will someone give me a hand here?"

One of the techs helped Alice move the body onto land. She then removed a pocket knife, slit open the back of the victim's pants and inserted a rectal thermometer. After about forty-five seconds, she removed it and checked the results. "At this point, the best I can tell is that our friend here has been dead for between eight and twelve hours. I'll do better once I get him to the shop."

She then inspected the laceration to the man's neck. "Cause of death was most likely from a deep, long incised neck injury to the front side of the neck. The left end of the injury started below the ear at the upper third of the neck and deepened—severing the left carotid artery and ending with a tail abrasion. Gentlemen, somebody cut this man's throat. Bag and tag him."

"When will you do the autopsy, Alice?" Marcus asked.

"Probably get started sometime tomorrow. Should have some preliminary information for you late Monday morning. But I can tell you this—whoever did this sure as hell knew what they were doing."

Two techs were in the process of putting the corpse in a body bag when Marcus said, "Hold on!" He moved closer. "Jesus Christ, Adam. Tell me I'm wrong, but that looks like the defense attorney at Demarco's trial."

Adam joined Marcus and said, "Son of a bitch, I think you're right." Adam found the tech who had the evidence bag and told him to pull out the wallet. One of the plastic holders had the driver's license in it. It was waterlogged and smeared, but the name was clear enough. "Holy shit, Marcus. Our corpse is Joe Wallace!"

# ABOUT THE AUTHOR

Geoff Collins holds graduate degrees in business and finance and a master's degree in education. He has held multiple management positions in Fortune 500 companies and was CEO of a Midwest advertising and public relations firm.

After a successful career in business, he taught elementary school for fifteen years. His passion for teaching reading and writing to his students led to a career as an author of both children stories and adult mysteries.

Geoff lives on Johns Island, South Carolina, with his wife, Sally. He has three grown children, Max, Leigh, and KC, and four grandchildren, John, Collin, Cora, and Lily.

# OTHER BOOKS BY
# GEOFF AND ART COLLINS

## *NIKKI AND THE TREE KEEPER*

*"What a wonderful and lovely tale!"*

*"Nikki is a heart-warming and inspirational story of finding your place in the world."*

*"Nikki and the Tree Keeper is magical."*

*"The illustrations are beautiful and add so much to the book."*

WWW.BOOKSBYCOLLINS.COM

# THE CHRISTMAS TOKEN

*"The Christmas Token is a heart-warming holiday tale about generosity, memories, and family."*

*"The artwork in this tender story is superior!"*

*"The Christmas Token should become a family tradition to read as the Christmas season begins!"*

*"Excellent!"*

*"Lovely book! My kids have read it many times over the holidays."*

www.booksbycollins.com

# THE ADVENTURES OF ARCHIBALD & JOCKABEB

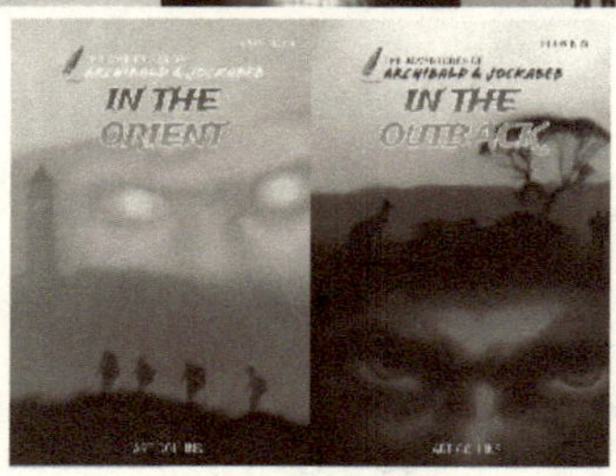

**"One of a kind!"**

*This is the best book EVER!!!!!! Dragons, Indians, horses, evil crows, there is nothing like it! I loved it … can't wait for more adventures to come.*

**"A majestic tale—*Harry Potter* meets *The Indian in the Cupboard*"**

*Loved reading these books. I quickly got hooked, dug in, and engaged with the characters. Wonderful stories.*

**"Rich in vocabulary!"**

*This book is rich in vocabulary. I can't wait to read all the other Archibald and Jockabeb books!*

**"Best of the best!"**

*In the Forest is an outstanding book! The characters are great and help make the wonderful story come together.*

**"Terrific series of action books!"**

www.booksbycollins.com

# *WHITE CLOUD AND THE GOLDEN CANYON*

*Excellent Native American tale for children and adults alike.*

*Wonderful life lessons for all.*

*Very enjoyable and true to our culture. (Akta Lakota Museum)*

www.booksbycollins.com

# THE BLACK CREEK MYSTERIES

Alex Foster and Travis Sanders live in a small southern Ohio farm town named Rivers Edge. Their first adventure takes them to the remote desert town of Sunshine, Arizona, where they find themselves in the middle of the Legend of the Apache Death Cave. The following summer, after Alex and Travis graduate from high school, they head to the small fishing town of Black Creek, Maine, for a relaxing vacation before they both head off to college. Their trip becomes anything but relaxing when they discover a mysterious creature in an underwater cave and a network of deadly gunrunners.

www.booksbycollins.com

# *THE MERCY KILLINGS*

**"A Holy City Mystery Artfully Spun"**

*Geoff Collins is a wonderfully versatile writer (check out his bibliography), and here, he weaves a delightful mystery set in the Holy City. Hop along and crack this case with Giordano—you won't regret, and it will get you primed for the other books coming along in the series.*

**"Well Written … Interesting Characters and Plenty of Suspense"**

*Good mystery with interesting characters and plenty of suspense. A cybersecurity expert is hired to determine if narcotics theft is taking place at Charleston SC hospital and who is behind it. Well written with lots of fascinating details.*

**"Wonderfully Crafted Story Set in Charleston"**

*Wonderfully crafted story set in Charleston, SC—great story line and vivid imagery. Collins follows Giordano with insight and honesty. Can't wait for Nick's next adventure.*

**"A Fast and Exciting Read"**

*The book was a fast read. It was exciting and held my interest throughout. Hope to see more from this author.*

www.booksbycollins.com

# *THE TOOLS OF THE TRADE*

Mario Rossini's Jersey syndicate, the Beltran-Lyve Cartel, and the KKK's Confederate White Knights are all battling for control over Charleston's drug trade. Nick Giordano and his friends once again find themselves entangled in the fight. And this time they may all be targets for the legendary Mafia hitman, Carlos Tucci.

**"Another Wild Ride"**

*Tools of the Trade takes us on another wild ride with Nick Giordano and his crew. Collins, as he did with his previous book in this three-part series (volume three is coming in 2019), deftly weaves on intricate story line that builds to a satisfying, thrilling end. Highly recommend Collins, a writer who deserves a vast readership.*

**"Excitement and Suspense"**

*Excitement and suspense as mafia and white supremacists fight over the drug market in Charleston SC. Characters well-developed and interesting story line.*

www.booksbycollins.com

# *SHARK BAIT*

Nick Giordano and his friends are drawn into the dark and dangerous world of the Russian mafia. The East Coast Russian mafia boss, Dimitri "The Shark" Pavlov, and his enforcer, Viktor Dudko, are using Charleston's Port Authority terminals for drug smuggling and human trafficking.

**"A Holy City Mystery Artfully Spun"**

*In this series, which sadly wraps here with Book Three, Collins found a higher gear with each, serving up a fresh batch of nasty folks for the series' core characters to root out and take down. That the books were set in Charleston only added to their delight. The only rotten aspect here is that this is the last we'll see of Nick Giordano and his pals—that is, unless, this crew comes around for cameos in one of Collins' future works. Hats off!*

www.booksbycollins.com

**Reading Partners** is a nonprofit literacy organization that recruits and trains community volunteers to provide one-on-one reading tutoring to students in under-resourced schools across the country. This highly effective program has helped thousands of children master the fundamental reading skills they need to succeed in school and beyond.

For more information, please visit www.readingpartners.org.

*"Literacy is not a luxury; it is a right and a responsibility. If our world is to meet the challenges of the twenty-first century we must harness the energy and creativity of all our citizens."*

*—President Bill Clinton*

www.ingramcontent.com/pod-product-compliance
Lightning Source LLC
Chambersburg PA
CBHW032121180726
48284CB00002B/653